CW00553491

PROWLED DARKNESS

A DANTE'S CIRCLE ROMANCE

CARRIE ANN RYAN

Prowled Darkness
A Dante's Circle Novel
By: Carrie Ann Ryan
© 2016 Carrie Ann Ryan
ISBN: 978-1-63695-083-9

PRAISE FOR CARRIE ANN RYAN....

"Carrie Ann Ryan knows how to pull your heartstrings and make your pulse pound! Her wonderful Redwood Pack series will draw you in and keep you reading long into the night. I can't wait to see what comes next with the new generation, the Talons. Keep them coming, Carrie Ann!" –Lara Adrian, New York Times bestselling author of CRAVE THE NIGHT

"Carrie Ann Ryan never fails to draw readers in with passion, raw sensuality, and characters that pop off the page. Any book by Carrie Ann is an absolute treat." – New York Times Bestselling Author J. Kenner

"With snarky humor, sizzling love scenes, and brilliant, imaginative worldbuilding, The Dante's Circle series reads as if Carrie Ann Ryan peeked at my personal wish list!" – NYT Bestselling Author, Larissa Ione

"Carrie Ann Ryan writes sexy shifters in a world full of passionate happily-ever-afters." – *New York Times* Bestselling Author Vivian Arend

"Carrie Ann's books are sexy with characters you can't help but love from page one. They are heat and heart blended to perfection." *New York Times* Bestselling Author Jayne Rylon

Carrie Ann Ryan's books are wickedly funny and deliciously hot, with plenty of twists to keep you guessing. They'll keep you up all night!" USA Today Bestselling Author Cari Quinn

"Once again, Carrie Ann Ryan knocks the Dante's Circle series out of the park. The queen of hot, sexy, enthralling paranormal romance, Carrie Ann is an author not to miss!" *New York Times* bestselling Author Marie Harte

DEDICATION

To my Readers.
Thank you loving this series even more than I thought possible.

ACKNOWLEDGMENTS

I can't believe its over. I started the Dante's Circle series years ago thinking it would be fun to write as many as paranormal creatures as possible. And yet each time I started a new book, I got to find so many new worlds, I knew I'd fall in love over and over again.

Thank you Kennedy Layne, Stephanie, Charity, Chelle, and Dr Hubby for helping me with Prowled Darkness. You guys pushed me to finish this one the way it should have been!

Thank you for following me through this journey and I hope you love this story as much as I do.

Happy Reading!

~Carrie Ann

PROWLED DARKNES

Eliana Sawyer's life was rocked from its foundation twice in as many years. She risked her heart and had it shattered into a thousand pieces when Malik left her with no warning. While she'd normally raise her chin and ignore the pain, she can't forget what he gave her before he disappeared from her life.

Malik Ward is a prince amongst the lion shifters and knows that one day he will have to take a mate. Only, his people can never mate with humans. Under the mistaken impression that Eliana was only human, he forced himself to leave before they'd crossed a line and he broke his vow to his people. Now that he knows the truth about Eliana, however, it will take more than groveling to win back the one woman fated to be his.

While Eliana and Malik embark on a new sensuous

path that might lead to disaster, the realms aren't ready to allow the final lightning-struck human to be enveloped into their fold. The couple will have to combat those plotting against them, as well as the broken promises and heated emotions they share.

Warning: Contains a Leo with a bite that's worse than his roar, a woman with one last chance at the life she's always dreamt of, a flame that could extinguish with the wrong sacrifice, and the final journey in the bestselling Dante's Circle series.

CHAPTER 1

Time changed in an instant. One minute, you're drinking a beer with your friends, talking about the increasingly scary storm outside; the next, you're flying through the air with your body slamming into the nearest wall when lightning strikes. Or rather, when lightning strikes *inside* the room and hits you and six of your friends dead center.

Eliana Sawyer's life changed the moment she felt the energy of the gods ricochet through her body. The world as she knew it became grey, and the things that went bump in the night became all too real. The paranormal world wasn't that of fiction anymore; now, she lived it. The way she saw the world, the way she saw life and fate changed. She couldn't plan a future the same way she had. She couldn't fall in love the way she'd thought to in the past.

After the lightning strike, six of her friends had found out the hard way what happened when they fell in love with someone paranormal—they became paranormal themselves.

Now, years later, here Eliana was—alone, all too human, and on the outside looking in.

Of course, she wasn't that alone anymore. She never would be again. While her friends had fallen for angels, demons, dragons, and wolves, she'd fallen for a mere human. A human that had taken her heart and shattered it into a thousand pieces, all the while leaving her with nothing but an echo of what he had once been, what they had once been together.

That wasn't the only thing he'd left her with.

He'd also left the life currently growing in her womb.

Eliana pressed her hands over her belly and tried to not think about everything that had happened in the past, and instead, worry about the future. Of course, the only thing she'd been doing for the past eight or so months had been worrying, but she couldn't seem to do anything else. Her emotions ran from excitement over the new baby because, damn it, she was going to be an amazing mother; to dread over the fact that she'd be doing this alone. The stops between the two emotions weren't picnics either.

Malik had left her high and dry with no way to contact him—going so far as to change numbers so his friend—and Eliana's friend's mate—Tristan couldn't even get ahold of him. Tristan had tried to reach out as soon as he'd heard about the pregnancy, but Malik was nowhere to be found. She didn't want to think about the fact that he'd so clearly cut all ties with the part of his past that was about her, but it was hard not to when the evidence of their relationship was currently doing a little dance on her bladder.

The little squirt tended to do that at all hours of the night. And the day for that matter. She'd heard stories from her friends about how some of them had sleeping little babies during their pregnancy. How those babies had been content to hang around and only perk up with a dose of caffeine. Yet her squirt was apparently a future soccer star.

Why wouldn't her baby be? It wasn't as if anything else in recent years had gone easily for Eliana, so why would this?

Little squirt decided to do one last kick straight to her bladder and Eliana winced. There would be no holding back the literal floodgates if she didn't get out of her chair and waddle her way to the bathroom. Whoever said pregnancy was a gift and women glowed during it clearly hadn't met her. Of course, maybe if she'd had a partner during it instead of freaking out all by herself, it would be different.

And that was enough of that. No more pity party. So what if Malik didn't want her and didn't know he was about to be a father. Or rather, a sperm donor since he'd actually have to *be* there to be a father. She'd do this on her own like she did everything else, and she'd live her life while trying not to ruin her baby's.

Easy.

She gripped the arms of her chair and tried to lever herself up. Only, when she made a grunting sound, nine men of varying sizes and species came at her, arms outstretched.

So maybe she wasn't so alone.

Since all six of her friends had found their mates and three of them had happened to find *two* mates, they didn't lack for men in their group. Only single men.

Eliana tried to wave them off but ended up wincing as little squirt did a summersault.

Seth was the closest to her and gave her a little grin.

She wanted to punch his face. Dimple and all.

"I've got you, Eliana," Seth said smoothly. He was a big man, all lean muscle and youthful features. He may be older than her since he was a merman and all, one who'd been around the block, but she was pretty sure she was the one who looked her age. He and Tristan had mated Amara around the time Eliana had found herself pregnant, and Seth had therefore declared himself keeper of Eliana.

One of many.

She hadn't missed the pitying looks on the others' faces. One of them was a ten-thousand-year-old dragon, but she could still see the sadness in his old eyes. They all felt sorry for her as if she were nothing but an incubator, all alone and manless. What they should have figured out was that plenty of women were single moms; she wasn't exactly an outlier.

Except for the tiny detail that she was the last lightning-struck without a mate, and therefore, human. Eventually, she'd start to age and the rest of them wouldn't. They'd pop out even more babies than they already had, and she'd have to watch as they made their families and thrived in new realms as well as the human one.

She'd die as a human while the rest of them mourned her.

But they'd be able to watch over squirt when she was gone. And squirt's children, too.

There may still be a chance that she'd find her mate, but it didn't mean fate would align for her perfectly. She was single and pregnant, so clearly fate had fucked with her already. If Malik hadn't been human, she would have thought he was the one for her. She hadn't had that same weird connection the others had felt, but he still could have been the one for her. He'd never met her friends since everyone had always been so busy with their own realms and she'd wanted to keep him to herself. Since he was human, she'd known he wasn't her mate, wasn't her true half, so it would have been weird to introduce him to a new world if he wasn't ready for it.

And, thankfully, she'd never trusted him with the secret of the paranormals since he'd clearly been on a different page than her.

"Eliana, honey, didn't you need to get up?" Seth somehow put his arms under her knees and behind her back and had her out of the chair and on her feet in the next instant. "What's wrong?"

She shook her head as Lily and Amara stood up as if to come closer. "I'm fine. Just thinking, and I have to pee." She inhaled through her nose and let out the breath. "Thank you."

With that, she waddled past Seth and the others, knowing if she didn't get out of there she'd make a fool of herself—and not just by peeing her pants.

She hadn't even closed the bathroom door before she heard the others start to speak about her. She might not have supernatural hearing, but it wasn't hard to figure out whom they were talking about.

The others had somehow gotten it in their brains that they needed to take care of her so they were all at Dante's Circle, the place where it had all started, to try to have a normal night. Most of them had babies with them or were pregnant.

Lily and Shade had their little Kelly, who wasn't so little anymore since she was walking and talking and going to an angelic preschool. Ambrose, Balin, and Jamie had Sami, who went to the angelic school with Kelly. Hunter and Becca had little Hazel, who kept wanting to shift into her little wolf form even in the human realm. Apparently, Hunter's dominance was helping her keep her shifting under control.

Dante, Jace, and Nadie were pregnant. Or rather, Nadie was, but her dragon and bear mates hovered like no other. If Eliana weren't so pregnant herself, she might have found humor in that. Faith and Levi weren't pregnant yet, but Eliana had a feeling it would happen any day now. The same with Amara, Tristan, and Seth.

It was scary to think that just a few short years ago, she and her friends had met up at the bar where Becca had worked, one that happened to be owned by a dragon, totally unaware of the inner workings of what truly went on around them. Now they were having babies, saving the world, and finding mates.

Eliana washed her hands when she was done letting the baby take care of her bladder and tried not to scowl at herself in the mirror. She didn't like acting as though she hated the world. She might not be as sweet-tempered as Nadie or soft-spoken as Lily, but she'd never been as...

hostile as Faith. She'd always figured she landed somewhere in the middle of the pack when it came to personalities. Not too harsh, but not too sweet.

Forgettable.

She closed her eyes and tried to push the doubt away. It wasn't easy when all she saw when she did was Malik's face when he'd kicked her out of his place. He hadn't physically touched her, but he might as well have thrown her away with the day's garbage.

She hadn't been good enough for him and, apparently, she'd just have to deal with it.

Eliana splashed some water on her face and let out a breath. "Stop it," she snapped at her reflection. "He's gone. He left you. So the fuck what? You're going to be a mom. So stop acting like a little fool and learn to be an adult."

"Some pep talk," Faith said from the doorway.

Eliana flipped her friend off and rubbed her back with her other hand. She was due in a couple of weeks, but the doctor had said it could be any day now. She wasn't ready for this, and no matter how many times she lied to herself saying she was, she never truly believed it.

"Your back hurt?" Faith asked as she moved toward her.

Eliana held out a hand. "I'm fine. Just the normal pain from lugging around squirt."

"Pain and fine don't usually go together," Faith said

dryly as she pushed her way toward Eliana. When her friend rubbed Eliana's back, tears sprang to her eyes.

Damn it. Malik should be the one rubbing her back. Malik should be the one making sure she was okay and trying not to comment on how swollen her ankles were.

Freaking hormones.

She let out a breath, annoyed with herself yet again. Malik wasn't here, but this baby was. She didn't know the sex because she'd wanted to be surprised, something out of character for her. Usually, she wanted to plan things perfectly, but since the baby wasn't planned, she'd wanted to keep it all in the same theme.

She wouldn't be alone for much longer; soon she'd be a mother. And no matter how much her heart hurt, no matter how much she wanted to scream or cry over the fact that she didn't have a clue what she was doing, she would be damned if she'd hurt this baby because of it.

This was *her* baby, and she'd love him or her until the end of days.

Faith leaned into her and Eliana held back a sigh. She loved her friends, she really did, but she knew once she had this baby, she'd be even more more separate from the rest. The others might not know it, but she did.

"Talk to me, Eliana," Faith whispered as she leaned into her shoulder, still rubbing her back. "What's going on in that head of yours?"

Eliana closed her eyes a moment before opening them

to meet Faith's gaze in the bathroom mirror. There was no use hiding from Faith. The other woman always seemed to know everything. In fact, all her friends did these days.

"I'm scared," she admitted.

"Of course, you are," Faith said simply. "If you weren't, I'd be worried about you."

Eliana raised a brow. "More worried than you already are?"

Faith shrugged and took a step back, keeping her hand on Eliana's back. "We love you. You can't lose us, even if you feel like you have to. I know you're scared about the baby and pissed off that that asshole Malik isn't here, but *we're* here. We're going to be kickass aunts and uncles, and you're not going to be able to get rid of us."

Eliana let out a watery snort. "Things are going to change, Faith."

"I know," Faith said softly. "They do every week it seems like these days." Her friend let out a breath. "I never really thought about what it would be like for the last of us."

Eliana blanked her face. She didn't want to hear what Faith had to say, but telling Faith what to do never ended well. Her mate, Levi, was about the only one who could really do it.

"We all knew our lives changed the day the lightning

struck," Eliana said coolly. If she let her emotions show, she'd break, and she wasn't ready for that.

"Yeah, and six of us have found our true halves. Six of us went through the agony of our first change and found our way into our new realms. I never thought about what it would mean for the seventh." Faith's eyes filled with tears and she quickly blinked them away. Eliana didn't want to see her friend cry. The woman rarely let emotions that could prove a weakness show.

"All it means is that I don't turn furry or have pink wings like you." She tried to smile as she said it, but Faith didn't even blink at the pixie joke.

"I'm not going to let you fade away, damn it. None of us are. I don't know what we're going to do, but you are *not* going to stay human." Faith crossed her arms over her chest and set her jaw.

"You really have no control over that." No one had control of anything.

Faith raised her chin. "Watch me."

And with that, her friend stormed out of the bathroom, and Eliana followed. Her ankles hurt and she wanted to sit down. Though her heart ached to think about what would happen when the others couldn't find a way to keep her with them in the long run, she pushed it aside. Little squirt deserved more than that.

She made it back to the table, and the others gave her solemn nods as if vowing something she wouldn't be able to control. But if that's what they needed to keep sane, then they could do it. It wasn't as if it would upset her more than she already was.

Seth handed her a glass of water and she grinned at him. "Thank you," she said. There. That was nice. Not the crazy pregnant chick.

"You're welcome. Do you need anything to eat? I can get you something." He was out of his chair before she could answer, hovering as if waiting for an order.

She couldn't help but laugh. "I'm fine, Seth. Take care of your mate. I won't break." She looked over at the others. "I won't break," she repeated. A vow of her own.

They nodded back at her and Tristan scowled before muttering something about fate under his breath.

Eliana sighed. "Fate had nothing to do with this, Tristan," she said calmly. "Malik was human. He wasn't my mate, wasn't my true half. He's gone now, and I'm going to be a mom. That's not fate. That's life."

Tristan froze, his jaw setting. "What did you just say?"

She blinked. "That's not fate. That's life?"

He shook his head, his hands shaking. "No, about Malik being human."

She didn't understand why he was acting this way. "Malik was human. Right? I mean, he's your friend and all."

Tristan cursed and stood up quickly, practically knocking his chair to the ground. "No. Malik is a lion shifter. He's in line for the throne. I thought you knew he wasn't human and that's why…fuck. Oh, fuck."

Eliana set the glass down on the table, afraid it would slip from her fingers. The others talked around her, asking her questions, speaking to Tristan as if he held all the answers.

"He…he never met any of you." She took a deep breath. "And I never mentioned…it's not like I have lightning-struck on my forehead or anything." Her eyes stung and she tried to focus. "He's a…he's a lion?"

"Why didn't you tell us?" Amara asked Tristan, worry on her face.

"Because I thought you knew!" Tristan scowled. "I swear to the goddess, I thought you all knew."

Dante shook his head and tapped his tongue ring to his lip. "None of us met him. I thought at one point I scented a lion on Eliana, but that could have been anyone." The dragon met Eliana's face. "While you were dating him, we didn't see much of you. None of us knew."

She tried to catch her breath. "So he's a lion. Okay. But that doesn't mean he's my true half. I didn't change into my paranormal self when he had sex like what happened with the rest of you. He didn't claim me as his. So he was just some random lion that left me. We aren't mates."

Tristan looked pained. "It's not that simple, Eliana."

She set her jaw. "Why? Why is the fact that Malik left me not simple?"

"Because lions don't mate the way other supernaturals do."

The hairs on the back of her neck rose at the sound of the deep voice behind her. She knew that voice. It haunted her dreams, and at one point, had made her shiver just from being softly spoken.

She slowly turned her head so she could see the man that had shattered her heart. His dark hair looked like it hadn't been cut since she'd last seen him, so long now it brushed his shoulders. His light brown skin stretched over thick muscles and she couldn't breathe at the sight of him.

"Malik," she whispered.

He glowered at her then let his gaze trail to her belly. "It seems we need to talk."

It seemed they did.

CHAPTER 2

There were times in a man's life when he felt like he held the world in his hands. There were times where that man could conquer that world and know instinctively what to do with the life it held.

This was not one of those times.

Malik Ward wanted to throw up, even though he didn't have a thing in his stomach. Or maybe yell at someone until he was so red in the face he couldn't speak. Perhaps hit someone so he could feel bone smash against bone. Or maybe, just maybe, go down to his knees in front of the woman who carried his child and beg for forgiveness.

As Malik was in line for the lion throne and a Ward, the latter wouldn't be happening.

Ever.

If he were anything less than the lion he was, he'd have tucked his tail between his legs and walked out of the bar as quickly as he'd come in. But he wasn't that kind of man, and now he had to face the consequences of his decisions.

And what consequences they were.

He'd been in his realm, trying to calm the rising storm and failing at everything he tried when he'd finally heard the full story of what had happened to Amara, Tristan, and Seth. If his head hadn't been so far up his ass, he'd have known why his friend had wanted to save his mates the way he had. Instead, Malik had been focused on his family and the realm that would soon be his because he hadn't had a choice in the matter.

He hadn't known Amara was lightning-struck—not until word had eventually spread that she was now the queen of the siren realm.

He hadn't known that Amara's friends were also lightning-struck. Therefore, he hadn't known that if those particular women found their mates, they would become the paranormal that held the most dominant strain in their DNA.

He hadn't known that the one woman he'd thought he could love—the one woman, if he let himself believe, he *did* love—was lightning-struck.

He'd kicked Eliana out of his bed, out of his life, and

had shut the door so tightly on that connection that he'd missed out on what could have been his future.

Holy. Hell.

Eliana was pregnant. With his child. His cub.

His mouth went dry and his brain fogged, much like it had when he'd first heard about what Eliana could be.

He hadn't known she was pregnant when he left. Hadn't known when he found out that Eliana could be his. He hadn't known until he'd walked in and almost fell to his knees. There was no doubt this was his child. Not with the timing or the way the others—and Eliana— glared at him as though he were the worst kind of person. He couldn't blame them, but he couldn't care about their opinions yet either.

Not until he spoke to Eliana and figured out what the hell they were going to do.

"You have a hell of a lot of nerve showing up here," a woman with dark hair and blunt bangs said. She stood up, and Malik scented pixie on her.

Well, that made sense since pixies were some of the most cutthroat paranormals out there.

"Faith, sit down," Eliana said, her voice strong. A hell of a lot stronger than he felt right then.

"You can't expect me to sit down while this asshole shows up after being missing for *months*." Faith waved her hand at him, and if she'd been in her full pixie form, he had a feeling her wings would have been red with anger right then.

The numerous others at the table began to speak at once. Even the babies cried or babbled in that baby language Malik had never been able to understand. His pulse pounded at his temple but he only had eyes for Eliana. He needed to speak to her, needed to explain, needed to find a way to breathe because he couldn't quite get enough air.

"Eliana," he whispered.

Eliana pressed her lips together and put her hands over her stomach, over *their* baby. He hadn't been here, didn't know until it was almost too late about the pregnancy, but the fact that she was carrying his cub changed *everything*.

The others became louder, even standing up to walk toward him. He stayed frozen to his spot, afraid to move closer and lose Eliana forever. Though, really, did he have her at all? He'd fucked up but it wasn't his fault. He'd done what he had to do with the evidence he'd held at the time.

"Stop it," Eliana said softly, though her voice was firm. "All of you. Sit down and take care of your babies. I need to speak with Malik. Alone."

She made a move to stand up, and he took a step toward her, needing to help, but stopped as a tall and slender man made it to her first. The other man glared over his shoulder at Malik as he put his hands on Eliana's arms.

"Thank you, Seth," Eliana whispered.

Seth. This was Tristan's mate, or at least one of them. That meant Malik didn't have to rip the man's arms off for daring to touch Eliana. He tried to keep his temper in check, fisting his hands at his sides and breathing through his nose. He had no right to feel this way, no right to fuck everything up once more. But it seemed the predator in him was ready to claim the woman in front of him. Hell, he'd been ready when he'd thought Eliana was human.

As lions couldn't mate with humans, he'd walked away.

Hopefully, Eliana would listen to him, would forgive him.

But he wouldn't grovel. He would one day be Leo and a Leo didn't beg.

No matter what might be needed.

"Eliana, let us go with you at least," Faith said.

"Let them be alone," Tristan put in, his eyes on Malik. This was his friend, or at least had been at one time. They weren't brothers, weren't warriors together, but they had once been closer than they were now. Endless time and responsibilities had separated them, but at least the man stood for him now. "For now," Tristan added, his eyes narrowing. "They should speak alone for now as they need to get the facts straight. But know this, Malik, if you hurt her again, you won't just have a pixie on your heels but also the rest of us."

"And we won't hold back for long," the large dragon said from the side.

Of course, Eliana was friends with a dragon. Why wouldn't she be?

Malik had never been so wrong in his life, and now he had to make sure he didn't lose her again. Because if he messed up, he had a feeling it would be the women at the table tearing him limb from limb, not the dragon or the fae in front of him.

Eliana pushed Seth's hands away and picked up her bag. "Let's talk then, Malik," she snapped. Fire slid into her eyes and he wanted to take a step back. He'd seen lionesses in a rage before, but he had a feeling they had nothing on a pregnant Eliana right then.

She moved past him, keeping her distance, and he let out a breath before following her. He didn't miss the glares sent his way, or the fact that the bear shifter at the table was casually sharpening his claws even in human form.

Dear goddess, this crew fought for their own like no other.

And while he liked the fact that Eliana had that—them —in her life, now that she was carrying his cub and he could be with her, she was *his* to protect. And once the others—as well as Eliana—understood that, things could go on like normal.

As he made his way to the sidewalk in front of Dante's Circle, he stopped by Eliana, who clutched her bag to her belly.

"You're going to need to drive as the others drove me here," Eliana said, her voice emotional. "I'm too big to fit behind the wheel safely."

He licked his lips as he studied her face. She was paler than he remembered, but that could have been from the shock of seeing him. Her shaggy red hair was longer now, brushing her shoulders in layers. When he'd last seen her, it had looked as though she could afford to gain a few pounds. Now, she was round with his child and had filled out nicely. He wanted to reach out and cup her face or even put his hand over her belly, but he didn't.

He didn't know what to do and that wasn't like him.

In fact, he hated it.

"Eliana…"

She held up a hand. "Not now. My ankles hurt and I have to pee. Again. I don't want to go back in there though because I don't think Tristan will be able to hold back the mob a second time. So, did you drive here? Or do we need to take a cab? Either way, let's go. We can go to my place because you sold yours." She raised her chin as he tried to process the fact that she'd been to his place after he left. Or rather, what had once been his place.

21

"Yeah, I went to your old condo. Sue me. I was trying to tell you about little squirt here. But whatever. So, cab or car?"

He blinked. "Little squirt?"

She pointed at her belly and raised a brow. "Car or cab?"

Apparently, she wouldn't be talking about any true details until they went to her place and he'd have to be fine with that. Because, frankly, his mind was still whirling over the fact that she was *pregnant*. He'd gone into the bar to find her so he could figure out what they were going to do about mating.

He'd never once thought she could be pregnant.

That changed everything.

And yet, it didn't change a thing.

He cleared his throat as she shuffled from foot to foot. Her ankles were hurting, she'd said. So maybe he needed to once again get his head out of his ass and take care of the woman carrying his child.

"I drove," he finally said. "Here, let me help you." He took her elbow, hopefully keeping her steady. He honestly didn't know what to do to help her. He may have been around some pregnant women in the Pride before, but he'd never really thought about how to help them beyond protection.

When she didn't pull away from him, he counted that as a small victory and led her to his Range Rover. She raised a brow at him when she saw the SUV, and he shrugged.

"I sold the Mercedes." He'd picked her up in that car when they were dating, and had sold it once he'd thought he would be spending the next few years with the Pride, working on his destiny. "I'm renting this."

She flinched slightly as he said it, and he wanted to curse at himself. Way to make it plain that he wasn't staying for long. And frankly, remind her that he'd left in the first place. He hadn't even *told* her that he wasn't staying, and yet the car sort of made that statement for him.

Instead of trying to explain, he helped her with her seatbelt and closed the door. He took steadying breaths as he made his way to the other side of the SUV and jumped in. This wasn't what he'd thought he'd be doing once he made his way back to the human realm, but now, he couldn't think of anything he'd rather do.

He had to fix this thing between him and Eliana. Because if he didn't, he wasn't sure what he would do.

They were silent as they made their way to Eliana's home. It wasn't lost on either of them that he remembered how to get there even if he'd never been to Dante's Circle before. He'd never actually been in her home as he'd never wanted to let things get too serious, but he'd picked her up from there numerous times. They'd only ever slept together in *his* bed. And his shower. And on his table.

But he'd never made love to her in her home.

He'd tried to keep that distance.

And, apparently, he'd fucked up in doing that. He'd fucked up in a lot of things with Eliana.

When he pulled into her driveway behind her beat up old truck, he barely had time to turn off the engine before she had her seatbelt off and was trying to wedge herself out of the Rover.

"Wait a minute," he snapped. "Let me help you before you get hurt."

"Too late," she whispered, and he cursed. "I've been getting out of cars on my own for a long time, Malik."

"But you don't have to do it alone now," he said, hoping she understood he meant more than just the vehicle.

She shook her head. "It's never as easy as that." But she waited for him to help her out of the Rover. That had to count for something.

His hands shook as she slid down his body, her belly protruding and scaring the shit out of him. When he felt a slight push at his own stomach, he froze.

Eliana blushed and tried to pull away from him. "That's just little squirt making his or her presence known. Just a kick. You don't have to freak out."

Malik's tongue went dry. He swallowed hard so he could speak. "It's my first kick," he whispered. Something else she'd said triggered his mind. "You don't know the sex of the baby?"

"I wanted it to be a surprise," she answered. "I don't know why now that I'm trying to figure out the nursery and everything. But I just went green and yellow." She shrugged. "And as for the kick? You could have felt them all if you'd been here, but you weren't." With that parting shot, she slowly made her way to the front door.

Malik let out a breath and closed the car door, locking it behind him. Well, he'd gone a little too fast just then, but it wasn't as if he'd done this before.

In fact, he wasn't aware of anyone who had this particular problem. It wasn't every day that a lion shifter next in line to the throne, dealing with a possible uproar and war in his Pride, found himself a soon-to-be father with a not-so-human potential mate after he'd left her all alone because he'd been forced to hurt her. There weren't any manuals for this sort of thing, so Malik was just going to have to wing it and pray to the goddess he didn't screw everything up.

Eliana let herself in and waved to the living room where there were two large chairs and a couch that looked lived in rather than ornate like the ones in his current home. He preferred these.

"Take a seat, I need to pee." With that, she left the room and walked toward a hallway that must go to the bedrooms. Malik ran a hand over his face.

Okay, as long as he didn't growl or roar, he should be okay. But telling a male lion not to be a lion wasn't exactly the easiest thing in the world.

He sank down into the cushions of the couch and tried to catch his breath. He was going to be a *father*. He'd barely had time to contemplate the fact that Eliana could be his because of her circumstances, and now there was a baby—little squirt—added to the mix.

He snorted at the nickname. That sounded like Eliana's doing and he liked it. A lot.

"What are you snorting at?" Eliana asked when she came back into the room.

Malik immediately got to his feet and walked toward her. She froze but didn't put her hand up to keep him away. "I was just thinking how much I like the name 'little squirt.'"

She blushed again but didn't say anything. It seemed she was waiting for him to speak or at least explain himself.

He sighed and reached out to cup her cheek. This time, she pushed him away. "Eliana."

"No. You don't get to do this. You can't just come back into my life after *crushing* me. I don't know why you had to leave, but I'm out, Malik. I'll let you say your piece, but I already made up my mind." Tears filled her eyes and she blinked them away. "I had to do that because of the baby and I can't just change it because you're back. It's not fair to me, and it's damn sure not fair to our child."

He shook his head. "I had to go, Eliana."

"You told me that it meant nothing to you. That *I* meant nothing to you."

He winced, remembering the words he'd been forced to say when he'd forced her out of his place. "It was the only way I could think of to shut you out of my life. I had to go. I know you don't understand, and I know I hurt you more than I can bear, but I hurt myself, too."

She flipped him off. "Boo hoo. You hurt yourself? Well, screw you."

He took her hand and kissed her middle finger. When she let out a growl of her own, he let her hand fall. "My kind, the lions, cannot mate with humans. It's not only forbidden, but the mating mark doesn't work. It's not prejudice, it's actually impossible. So when I started to fall in love with you—" She opened her mouth to speak, and he put his fingers over her lips. "Let me finish. When I started to fall in love with you, I knew I had to leave because it would hurt us more in the end. Or, at least, that's what I thought. I didn't know you had a chance to shift into something paranormal. I didn't know *we* had a chance."

She shook her head, this time letting a tear fall down her cheek. He brushed it away with his thumb and tried to catch his breath.

He wouldn't grovel, wouldn't fall to his knees and beg forgiveness. He was the son of the Leo, the King of all lions. He would, one day soon, be the Leo and reign over his people. He couldn't fall for her more than he already had, but he could hope she could see how he felt.

Because if she didn't, he wasn't sure what he would do next.

CHAPTER 3

E liana couldn't quite believe what he was saying. And yet, she knew he wasn't saying everything she needed to hear. There were a few key things missing from his speech, and she wasn't sure she could forgive him without those words.

In fact, he hadn't asked for forgiveness at all.

He was just so...*male*.

A male lion, at that.

The king of the freaking jungle was an asshole.

"You know none of that matters, right?" she said, her voice cracking. "Because there's no tug or anything like the other girls had." Amara hadn't felt it, but that had been a siren curse and Eliana had a feeling that wouldn't happen twice. "I can't be your mate because I didn't shift into my paranormal self the first time we had sex. That's how things work for the lightning-struck. That's how it's always worked. I'm not your mate."

And it hurt more than she could bear that she'd been forced to say that, been forced to come to that conclusion long before he'd returned to her life.

"You'll be the father of this baby because I'm not so callous as to push you away from him or her, but you'll never be mine." She swallowed hard. "You can't be."

Malik cupped her face and shook his head. "That might be how the other paranormals and lightning-struck work. But that's not how lions work."

"What do you mean?" She remembered now that he'd said something like that when he'd walked into Dante's Circle, but her mind had gone in so many directions since then that she'd forgotten. "How do lions mate?"

"We choose," he said simply.

"Huh?"

His thumb caressed her cheekbone, and it took all within her not to turn into his palm and nuzzle him.

"As lions, we don't give in to fate like the others. There isn't some magical connection that sparks between a lion and his mate. That comes after. The lion within chooses a mate, and the human half almost always agrees. We *choose* a mate. Meaning, the bond doesn't come from sex alone, and you wouldn't have shifted into your paranormal self because there wasn't a bond yet. And before you ask, I didn't let the bond happen—though my lion wanted you—because I thought you were human. I didn't know it *could* happen at all."

She let out a shaky breath and her knees went weak. If she weren't forty-seven months pregnant, she might not have almost fallen as she had, but with little squirt doing somersaults the same way her heart was, she couldn't keep her body up.

Malik caught her easily and lifted her into his arms. Alarm spread over his face as he carried her to the couch. His muscles didn't even look strained from carrying her weight, and she had to give it to the gods who had developed lion shifters. Because, damn.

"What's wrong? Is it the baby? What can I do? Do you need water? What about sheets? Is the baby coming?"

His hands were actually shaking on her, and she had to hold back a smile. "I'm fine. Really. I just got a little lightheaded over everything. The baby isn't coming." To emphasize the fact, little squirt kicked again, and Malik's eyes widened.

"That was a foot," he coughed. "I just saw a foot."

She put her hands on her belly and nodded. "Kicking seems to be his or her pastime. It's like I'm incubating a little alien baby or something."

Malik blinked, his face pale. "Not an alien, a lion cub."

She froze. That made sense. As with the others in her group, the dominant strain of DNA would be the one to lay claim to the baby's abilities. Thousands of years ago, as the supernaturals mated with one another over and over, the bloodlines became so diluted a new race was born—humans. It was because of that, that certain members of the Conclave—the governing body of the paranormals—had tried to see what would happen if something sparked the dormant paranormal DNA in some humans.

Hence, Eliana and her friends.

Since lion shifter outweighed whatever fraction of paranormal DNA Eliana had left within her body, the baby would be a cub. A lion cub.

Dear goddess.

In all her planning for the baby, she hadn't thought about birthing a baby shifter. What would she do? Would it come out in shifter form? No, the others' hadn't, but what if she were different? Could a human birth a lion? What if the baby clawed its way through all the new furniture Eliana had bought?

Her mind went dizzy again, and Malik held her to him.

This was all too much. And yet, the man hadn't asked for forgiveness.

He'd assumed she'd be there at his side, and yet she couldn't breathe, couldn't figure out what she would do next. Eliana was more than that.

"I can mate with you now, Eliana. We can go on like

we should have in the first place, like none of this ever happened."

That was the wrong thing to say. Holy hell, this man would never learn.

She let out a breath and cupped his face before raising her lips to his. He let out a shocked gasp before kissing her back. His lips were smooth yet firm. She loved his lips, loved the way they felt on all parts of her.

And yet, there was a chance she wouldn't have those lips on her again.

Because she was worth more than what he was giving her, and if he didn't understand that, then there wasn't a future for them.

"I can't do this, Malik," she whispered.

He pulled back, confusion in his gaze. "What do you mean? You're not human. We can mate and raise this baby and everything will be okay."

She shook her head. "It's not that easy, and if you would stop thinking like a prince of the lions or whatever, you'd see that. You can't come back into my life after being gone for *months* and tell me that I'm yours and everything is okay."

"What do you mean? I'm not pushing it under the rug, but I'm here now. We can move on."

She let out a growl and pushed him away, this time not stopping the tears from falling down her cheeks in force. "You *left* me. You made me feel like I'd done something wrong or that I wasn't good enough. You made it so I couldn't get ahold of you when I found out I was pregnant. Even your so-called friend Tristan couldn't reach you because you'd hidden within your realm."

"I had reasons, I had to leave."

"And you haven't told me them. You just told me that you couldn't have me so you left and broke me in the process. So unless you have something else to say, I can't be with you. I can't put myself out there without finding a way to trust you again." She paused and rested her hands on her belly. The baby gave a soft kick, as if knowing she needed the touch. "I can't let you be with me, and I can't be with you only because the baby is now part of the equation."

"That's not what I'm saying," he growled. "I'm here because of you. I came back to the human realm because of you. The baby just made it that much more imperative."

She shook her head. "You still don't get it. You can't dictate."

"I'm not dictating. I'm saying you'll come with me to the lion realm and we'll raise this baby together and be mates. There isn't another option because it's what we both want. I don't understand why you're not more excited about this."

She blinked. He truly didn't get it. She didn't think he was being callous or even cruel. He just simply didn't understand that she needed more than words about a fate she'd never fully trusted. She needed him to know that he'd hurt her and to find a way to make that better because there would be no healing until he understood that. She couldn't raise her baby with him without the assurance that he wouldn't leave again.

Or worse, take the baby with him.

He hadn't said as much, and she *knew* she was overreacting to that end, but she couldn't think with him so close...so close, and yet, so far away.

"I need time to think, and you're not giving me time. You're telling me what we're doing because that's what you're used to. I don't know how your realm works, but I know enough about lions in the wild to know that you think you're the king of the jungle. Or at least something like that."

"I'm not a lion in the wild," he growled.

"And I'm not a lioness or prey. I'm a pregnant human who is freaking out over the fact that everything I thought was real isn't. You're not human. This *baby* isn't human. And now you're *telling* me I'm your mate and we're going to live happily ever after in your realm. You didn't ask. You didn't even *think* about the fact that I have a job here. I have friends here. Family. I had to make plans when you left, and you can't rip them all away because you think you're back and my king. It doesn't matter that you're a shifter when it comes to that. I wouldn't let *any* man dictate my life. Now, you need to go so I can think."

"I'm not leaving you and our baby." He held onto her arms but didn't squeeze. He knew his own strength, and she had to give him praise for that. He wouldn't hurt her physically, but he'd damned sure hurt her emotionally before.

"You need to go," she whispered. "Give me time." He hadn't admitted that he'd done anything wrong. Hadn't said he was sorry for breaking her. Hadn't given her a second thought, beyond bringing her with him to his realm. He might have said he was falling in love with her, but he hadn't said anything else along those lines. If she had to beg for him to grovel, then it wasn't a true grovel. She didn't need to see him on his knees, that wasn't who she was, but she needed him to give her time.

"I don't want to leave you," he whispered.

"You did it before." It wasn't fair of her to say so, but she wasn't feeling very fair at the moment.

He swallowed hard. "I'll be back soon. Once…once you have time to think." He cupped her face. "I…" He didn't finish his sentence. It was as if he couldn't, and she wasn't sure what he would have said anyway. Instead, he kissed her forehead and walked away.

She'd been the one to push him away this time, yet it hurt just as much as it had before. The door clicked closed behind him, and she gasped out a sob, her body shaking. Why had she said what she'd said? Why had she pushed him away like that?

It made no sense. The only thing she wanted was to wrap her arms around him and never let him go.

And that was why she didn't do it.

Because once she did, she'd never let go. And she wasn't sure she'd survive if she had to watch him leave her again. He might have said they could mate and he could mark her—not that she knew what that entailed since she hadn't asked and he hadn't offered up an explanation—but she wasn't sure she could trust that. This wasn't like the movies where the hero would walk in and say she was his and the heroine would fall into his arms, happy and forgiving without another word. There weren't happy endings in real life. Not entirely. Not without work and words that meant something. Eliana hadn't heard those words from Malik, and she hadn't given them to him either.

She needed a moment to breathe, to figure out what to do next about her and little squirt. Having Malik around, hovering like the male he was, wouldn't allow her to think. Of course, she hadn't merely said that to him. She'd lashed out because she was still hurt.

And that was something she'd have to apologize for once he came back.

If he came back.

The door opened again and she lifted her head, her heart in her throat. Had he come back already?

When Amara walked in, her long auburn hair in curls around her face, Eliana let out another sob. Her friend rushed to her side, wrapping her arms around Eliana's shoulders. Eliana leaned in to Amara and let the grief that she'd done a poor job of hiding so far slide over her. She'd let Malik walk away—forced him to go away—because she hadn't been able to deal with the feelings inside of her. She knew she should have let him stay and say more, but if she had, she might have given in without thinking of herself and her child. It might be the right choice in the end, but Eliana still feared that she'd made a horrible mistake.

"Shh, darling, let it out," Amara whispered. "You haven't let yourself do this in all these months."

Eliana swallowed hard and wiped her face even as more tears came. "I haven't been able to. I was afraid I'd never stop." She sniffed hard. "And now I don't think I can."

"You can, and you will when you're ready. Why don't you tell me what Malik said and what you thought about it."

"How did you know I'd need you?" she asked before she began.

"We all wanted to come, even the guys, but I said I would be the one to be by your side tonight." She cupped

Eliana's face and kissed her brow. "I was where you are. Before." Her friend winced. "Okay, not exactly where you are, but remember? I thought I was crazy for wanting Seth and Tristan like I did, and no matter what we did, we couldn't mate because of the curse."

Eliana nodded and sighed. Amara had had to kill the siren queen in order to keep her men and survive. In fact, each of Eliana's friends had gone through hell—sometimes literally—when they'd found their mates and figured out how they would live in a new world that wanted nothing to do with them.

She wasn't alone, but she wasn't the same as the others. Though they were each as unique as the realms that had claimed them.

"This sucks," she said simply, and Amara snorted out a laugh.

"That it does. So, tell me, dear pregnant friend, what happened?"

Eliana let out a sigh once more and leaned in to her friend's embrace, keeping her hands on her belly so she could be close to little squirt.

"Malik didn't know I was his mate because lions apparently can't mate humans. He left because he had responsibilities." She paused. "He said he was falling in love with me and didn't want to make promises he couldn't keep, so he pushed me away and left. As soon as he found out I was lightning-struck, he came back and

39

found out I was pregnant. And now, everything will be swept away and he will mate with me, mark me or whatever, bring me back to his realm, and be king of the lions and we'll raise our baby in perfect accordance with whatever dream he has in his head."

Amara was silent for so long that Eliana had to turn and look over her shoulder.

"What?" Eliana asked. "I told him to go because he didn't apologize for leaving. He didn't tell me what he felt now. He just told me what would happen and expected me to go alone with it."

"He's a dude," Amara said. "I'm mated to two of them. They don't always understand that they need to explain things and listen."

"That's a little sexist," Eliana said, though she'd thought the same thing already.

Amara rolled her eyes. "Let me rephrase then. He's a dude who is friends with my Tristan. So, yeah, he is an idiot when it comes to communication. They all were— still kinda are. And frankly, so were we when I think about it. He needs to apologize, yes. And he needs to listen to you and take steps *with* you rather than *for* you. But he's hurting too, honey. Can't you feel that?"

Eliana pressed her lips together. She'd seen the hurt in his gaze, but she couldn't see past her own. And that was wrong.

"I have to be strong for the baby," Eliana said softly. "I

can't just use the excuse that 'well, Daddy had to be the king, young Simba, so I gave up everything.'"

Amara let out a snort. "Please don't name your baby Simba or Nala."

Eliana laughed. "No Mufasa or Scar either." She closed her eyes. "Dude. I'm going to have a baby. A baby cub. What the hell am I going to do?"

Amara hugged her close and kissed her temple. Her friend warmed her when Eliana hadn't been sure she could ever feel any form of warmth again. "You're going to be a kickass mom. You and Malik are going to talk and figure out a plan. Whether you are together or apart, you'll be there for this baby. We all will. I know fate just threw you a curveball of epic proportions, but you can handle it. You're stronger than you think you are."

Eliana hoped her friend was right. Because everything had changed once again and now she had to be the rock for not only herself but her baby, as well. Only she was tired of being the rock. She wanted to lean against someone. She wanted a partner.

She just didn't think Malik knew what it meant to be a partner.

Because she sure as hell didn't.

CHAPTER 4

M alik had made a colossal mistake, and he only
had himself to blame. He shouldn't have left her
alone in the house. He shouldn't have left to begin with.
Yet, no matter what, he couldn't go back to either time
and make a different decision.

What he *had* to do, was be a fucking adult and own up
to his mistakes. Because by brushing it all away and
trying to only think of the future without asking about
the past, without dealing with it at all, he'd messed up
royally.

He'd been so worried about not falling to his knees
because of how he'd been raised, that he'd let the one
person in the world who could truly be his slide through
his fingers. As a lion shifter, he might not have the same

fated mate idea like the others in the realms around him, but his lion had already chosen Eliana.

He should have listened to the damned cat when he had the chance.

Now, he was alone in his Rover, driving around like a freaking idiot because he didn't have a home in this realm anymore. He couldn't go to the one friend he knew was near because Tristan would kick his ass for hurting Eliana in the first place.

He was alone, and he was the only one to blame.

Malik should go back and beg for forgiveness. He should fucking grovel and ask Eliana to be his. He should *listen* to her and see what she needed, rather than proclaim that they would be mates in a realm that was as foreign to her as a new world.

His knuckles turned white on the steering wheel as his grip tightened. Enough of this. Self-pity wouldn't help anyone. The only thing he could do was go back to Eliana and say his piece in truth. She might want space, and he would give it to her, but first, he needed to do the one thing he should have done in the first place.

Recognize her agony.

He did a U-turn and sped back to her place, praying he wasn't too late—and that he wouldn't get pulled over. Luckily, no one stopped him until he made it to the front door of her home, his arm raised to knock.

He froze, scared out of his mind.

What if after he'd spoken to her, after he'd told her that he loved her, she pushed him away again? What would he do? He let out a growl and cursed at himself. This was why there was even an issue in the first place. Time to nut up and be a fucking man about the fact that he loved the woman in that house, and the fact that he was going to be a damned father.

The door opened before he could knock and he swallowed hard at the sight of Tristan's mate, Amara on the other side.

"You came back," Amara said as she narrowed her eyes. "Good. Now don't fuck up again because if you do, I'll show you *exactly* what it means to be a siren."

"You can't kill him, Amara! Don't sing his song!" Eliana called from the living room, and Malik had to swallow hard. Again.

"Please don't sing my song," he said gruffly. "I'll make this work. I promise."

Amara shook her head. "It's not me you should be making promises to and you know it. Now, I'm going to leave and see my mates, and you are going to fix this by being honest. I know you're scared, and you should be, but don't hurt my friend or I will end you. Got me?" And with that, the sweet-looking siren pushed past him and headed toward the other car in the driveway that he hadn't even noticed was there when he'd pulled in.

"You're back," Eliana said as she moved toward him.

Her eyes were puffy and her cheeks were red, but she'd stopped crying.

"Your friend scares me," he said honestly. It was the first thing to come to mind, and once it was out, he wasn't sure if he should have said it at all.

Eliana laughed. "Yeah, she scares me, too. In fact, all my friends do now. They're powerful and protective but they're mine. Are you going to come in, or are you going to stand in the doorway for the rest of the evening?"

He moved in quickly, closing the door behind him. "Eliana."

"Before you start, I wanted to say I'm sorry."

He blinked. "Why are you sorry? I'm the idiot."

She snorted. "I won't say you're wrong there, but I'm sorry anyway. I shouldn't have pushed you away while we were trying to talk. It was all too much for me and I just reacted." She put her hands on her belly. "No matter what happens between us, we're connected because of this baby. I don't want to be with you *only* because of the baby, but I didn't really give you a chance to talk about that at all. Instead, I freaked out and tried to hurt you like you'd hurt me. And for that, I'm sorry."

He went to her quickly, cupping her face and tilting her head so he could see her eyes. Her skin was soft and warm beneath his palm, and all he wanted to do was nuzzle her and purr. He was a cat, after all.

"I am the one who should be sorry. I hurt you, Eliana.

I hurt you and I hurt myself. But I thought I knew what I was doing. I left you and I shouldn't have. Both times. I also shouldn't have, like you said, dictated our future. I should have listened even as I tried to explain. I'm going about this all wrong and all I can think of as an excuse is that I'm scared to death because I've never done this before."

Eliana closed her eyes and leaned in to his palm. He could have purred once again. "I hope you haven't done this before," she teased.

He leaned forward and kissed the tip of her nose. She opened her eyes, and he knew he could get lost in them forever. She was his, even if he had to find a way to start from scratch and ensure she knew he could be hers, as well.

"I want to be your mate, Eliana. I want to raise our child together in whatever realm you feel at home in, but I want to be by your side."

"I'd love that," she whispered. "But we also have to figure out who we are together with everything out in the open. We fell into the relationship we had before because we each thought the other was human, and that changes how we are now. Does that make sense?"

He nodded and leaned forward again, taking her lips softly. She moaned into him and he had to pull back before he moved too fast, too soon.

"I don't know how far back to go to start over. I think

we're past the introduction part." He moved one hand to her belly, and she smiled.

"Maybe just a little introduction?" She took a deep breath, and he had to brace himself, afraid of what would happen once they got past this. "I'm Eliana. I'm a welder and artist, though right now, I'm preparing to be a mom. A few years ago, the Conclave struck my friends and me with a special type of lightning, and now, one day, when I find my mate and sleep with him during our mating, I'll change into whatever paranormal creature holds the strongest part of my DNA. I have no idea what that will be, as each of my friends before me has turned into things I never dreamt of. I'm pregnant with your child and I'm scared to death that you're going to leave again because I don't know how to trust people." She licked her lips. "Your turn."

He chuckled roughly. "I'm Malik Ward, prince of the lion realm. My father is the current Leo. He's also dying." Eliana let out a pained breath, and he kissed her cheek. "I had to leave the one person I knew I could fall in love with so I could care for him. I also left because I was afraid if I fell fully, I wouldn't be able to keep her because I thought she was human. Now my father is dying and my uncle wants the throne even though I'm next in line. So I've spent the past few months reassuring the Pride that I am who they need me to be and that I can rule as their leader. But all the while, I've wanted to be with the one person I couldn't be with. As soon as I found out about Amara and thereby you, I came here. I came to take you with me, but I know that was wrong. I should have come to tell you everything, rather than assume you'd want to be mine at all." He paused. "And now we're going to have a baby and I'm scared as all hell but excited." He smiled despite himself. "We're going to have a baby," he repeated.

"I didn't know about your father," she whispered. "I'm so sorry, Malik. Are you close to him?"

Malik shook his head. "Not as close as I'd like to be. I've spent the past few years away from the Pride, roaming. I'm not as old as Tristan, by the way. I'm only thirty-eight." He grinned when her eyes widened. "Lions are long-lived so I'm relatively young, hence why my uncle wants the throne. The only reason my father is dying is because he was poisoned years ago in a fight to protect the Pride. It's just now taking its full toll on him."

"I'm so sorry, Malik." She wrapped her arms around him as much as she could with her belly between them, and he let his shoulders relax for the first time in a long while.

He cleared his throat. "Before we talk more, though, I should probably tell you that another reason my uncle is trying to declare me unfit is that I don't have a mate." He winced. "So I had planned to go to the Pride and find a lioness because that was my duty."

Eliana took a step back and he felt the coldness sweep over him at the lack of her touch. "Excuse me?"

He held out his hands. "I didn't do it. I couldn't. I had you in my mind, under my skin. You were it for me and I couldn't go through with whatever plan the others might have had for me. I also don't want you to think that you have to mate with me for me to be the Leo or anything. Because I want what happens between us to be about *us* not what the others want."

Eliana closed her eyes. "That is…that is a lot."

"I know. And I should have told you that to begin with but I fucked it up when I first got here. I think that's all, Eliana. I mean, there is so much more to me than what I said, and I know there is more to you, but that's a start, isn't it?"

He went to his knees, a future Leo in love with the woman before him. "Forgive me, Eliana. Be with me. Be my mate and let me show you my realm. I know it's fast and I know we still have to figure out who we are, but be with me."

Eliana tilted her head. "Will having a mate help you with your Pride?"

He frowned. "Yes, but—"

"Then I'll help." She raised her chin. "I'm not going to put my baby or you in danger because your uncle wants your role. I take it you want to be Leo?"

He blinked. "It's all I've ever known." He paused. "And

yeah, I want to be Leo. I know I can do good for my Pride. But Eliana, I don't want you to mate with me because you're trying to protect me. I want you to be with me because you want to."

She pressed her lips together. "I want you, Malik. I always have and that was the problem." She put her hands over her belly once more. "I want this baby to come into a world where he or she knows they're loved. I...was falling for you before, too, Malik and I think that if we stay together, if we are together, I will fall for you irrevocably." She met his gaze. "But I want to mate with you. I want to take a chance with fate because I've never taken a chance like that before. Can you do that? Can you be with me? Can I trust you?"

He cupped her face. "I want to be with you, Eliana. You *are* my mate as I am yours. My lion chose you long ago, and I choose you, as well. But I need to hear the words. I need to know you want to be mine because of who we are, not because of a chance. You can trust me, Eliana. I didn't have all the facts before and I left. I shouldn't have, but I didn't know any better. I will forever be sorry for that, but I can't mate with you if you don't want me like I want you."

She closed her eyes and a tear fell down her cheek. "I was just using the fate crap as a shield and I didn't do a very good job with it." She met his gaze. "I want you as mine, Malik, and I'm scared. So scared that if I don't mate with you now that I'll lose you forever. Be with me, Malik. Please."

He couldn't ignore her words, couldn't say no. So instead of dealing with more of the emotions that could take over his mind and his heart, he pressed his lips to hers in a promise. He loved her, and he knew that if she opened her heart, she could love him, too. He would mate with her, be with her, and show her the man he could be. They'd deal with the Pride, her friends, and whatever realm her new life would fall into once they were mated and she was his.

His lion couldn't hold back anymore and, frankly, neither could he.

She moaned into him and he growled softly. His hands went to her sides and down her stomach. When he pulled back, they were both breathless.

"I've never made love to a pregnant woman before," he breathed. "Can you at this stage? Will I hurt either of you?"

She shook her head. "My doctor told me I could, though I never really thought I would." She blushed and he cupped her face.

"I have a better idea," he growled, though his cock was hard as a rock. "I can mark you as mine. It's a bite on your shoulder that marks you as a lion's mate. It will fade over time, but all lions will know it's there. It's how lions mate. The sex is usually a bonus."

She chuckled. "So you'd bite me and we wouldn't have sex."

He kissed her softly. "I think we both need time to get to know one another before we make love again. I don't want to rush things."

"But mating us so we're connected for all eternity isn't rushing things?"

He scrunched his face. "I didn't say I made any sense."

She sighed. "I know what you mean. I know you're mine and I can't explain it, so letting you bite me so I'm yours forever makes sense to me. But...I kind of like waiting for the physical part of our relationship. Are we crazy?"

"Yes," Malik said instantly. "Crazy as hell, but I'm okay with that."

Eliana nodded. "Okay, then. So you bite me and we're mates. Then what?"

"Then I make you dinner?" he asked, rather than answered. "Or we go to your friends. Or the Pride. I'm not exactly sure. But we'll do it together. No more running." That was a promise he knew he'd fight like hell to keep. He'd deal with the Pride in his own time. He'd have to return home soon to deal with his father, but he hoped, this time, Eliana would be by his side.

"There's a chance that I'll change if this is the way mating works for you," she said suddenly.

He cursed. "I know, and we'll deal with that. I'm yours, Eliana. I'll be with you no matter what."

She didn't say anything and he knew he deserved that. He'd win back her trust one day, even if it took him until his last breath. She was worth that and so much more.

"Where are you going to bite me?" she asked.

"Your shoulder," he repeated.

"I mean, in the house. Do you want me in the bedroom? Or right here? Do you need music or something?"

He smiled and rested his hand on her belly. The baby kicked him and a smile spread across his face. "We can go to the couch, Eliana. We can do this slowly and I'll show you that you're mine. You and little squirt here."

"Okay, then," she breathed and took his hand, leading him to the couch.

He sat down next to her and pulled her hair away from her face, pushing it over the opposite shoulder. He loved the slope of her neck, the curves on her body. He loved everything about her. And maybe, one day soon, she'd believe that. He never thought he'd be so lucky as to have her for his—and he'd almost lost it all.

"Will it hurt?" she asked, a little bit of fear in her voice.

"No," he answered before licking her neck. She let out a moan, and he couldn't help but grin in satisfaction. "My bite will feel like pure bliss."

"Bite many women, have you?"

He licked again. "Only you, Eliana. Only ever you." And with that, he bit down. She gasped before reaching out to hold his arm.

He wrapped her hair around his fist and kept his bite firm and still so he wouldn't hurt her in any way. His lion roared, scratching at him, wanting out so he could have their mate in their arms.

The bond between them snapped into place, a thread of pure joy, promise, and heat. He let his fangs slide out of her skin and threw back his head, letting out a roar that spoke of his line, his duty, and his mate.

Eliana's grip on his arm tightened and he lowered his head so he could kiss her, taking her as his.

Only he couldn't.

Instead, her eyes widened and her body glowed a fiery red and gold. She let out a silent scream and clutched her stomach with her free hand.

"Eliana!"

Flames skittered around her body but didn't burn him; instead, the warmth calmed his cat and he tried to figure out what to do next. His mate was changing…her body becoming who she truly was rather than the woman she thought she had to be.

And she was his.

He just prayed this wasn't the end.

CHAPTER 5

Eliana wasn't dying, but damn if it didn't feel close to it. Her fingers burned, her chest burned, her legs burned, and if she thought about it, her hair burned. She threw her head back and screamed, begging the goddess or whoever was out there to make the pain stop.

The others told her it had hurt for a few moments when they'd first changed into their paranormal selves, and that they'd sparkled a bit before passing out or ending up with wings.

For some reason, Eliana didn't think either of those things was happening to her.

Instead, she was on *fire*.

Maybe she was a dragon like Dante. That would be kind of cool because he was kickass, but she wasn't sure she could deal with the unknowing for much longer.

She put her hand on her belly once more, praying the baby would be okay. What had she been thinking risking this when she was pregnant? If the baby got hurt because of hers and Malik's actions, she'd never forgive herself.

Then, as suddenly as the flames had appeared, they faded away and she fell against Malik's chest, trying to catch her breath. His hands roamed her body as if checking for wounds, but she didn't think he'd find them. The fire hadn't been normal, and while he'd touched her when she'd burned, he hadn't been in pain.

The fire hadn't harmed them even though it had practically consumed her.

"Eliana? Are you okay? The baby? What do you need?" His voice got rougher with each word, and she figured it was the cat coming closer to the surface. The same thing happened with Hunter whenever he got emotional or agitated over Becca and the baby.

She let herself lean on Malik a bit longer, his scent and hard muscles a comfort. When she pushed at his chest slightly, he tightened his grip on her for a moment before letting her go.

"I'm okay," she rasped. She cleared her throat and took a deep breath. The baby kicked and seemed content. She sighed. "And the baby's okay." She met Malik's gaze. "We're okay."

Malik cupped her face and brought his lips to hers in

a gentle caress before pulling away only to lean his forehead on hers. "You scared the life out of me."

"Good thing cats have nine lives, then," she teased. If she didn't laugh, didn't try to make things okay, she'd start to freak out. She hadn't looked down at herself yet to try and see if she could figure out what she'd turned into. Maybe she wouldn't recognize herself, or maybe she'd be something that would scare her to death. She'd known transforming would be a possible side effect of the bite, but she'd been so wrapped up in the thought of forever with Malik that she'd gone into it without truly thinking.

She'd wanted to believe in him and herself, so she'd taken the leap.

And now, she and the baby would have to deal with the consequences.

"What am I?" she asked after Malik had snorted at her comment.

"You are mine," he answered roughly, his forehead still on hers.

She closed her eyes, wanting to roll around in those words for a lifetime. "Malik." Her voice was soft, pleading.

"You are a phoenix, Eliana. A beautiful, unique, and rare phoenix."

She pulled away, her eyes wide. "Seriously? A *phoenix*? That's a thing?"

He gave her a half-smile, worry evident in his gaze. "Yes, beauty, it's a thing. A rare one, like I said, but not unheard of. I've only met one phoenix in my life, in fact, as they tend to stay within their own realm, but you carry the markings and scent of one."

She blinked. "Scent?"

"Like burnt amber over spun sugar," he explained. "The sweetness is all your own, but the amber is that of the phoenix. Other species can carry something similar, but nothing is as pure as that of a phoenix."

She couldn't quite process what it all meant and what would come, but she would. "Why do you seem so worried?"

He cupped her face before putting the other hand on her belly. "Because you can die, my love."

She paused at his endearment but worried more about his words. Slowly, she said, "I think you need to tell me what you know about phoenixes and what I can do. Because we all can die, Malik, but you're worrying me. Is the baby okay?"

He nodded. "The baby should be fine. I mean, I don't think the transformation would have hurt him or her, but we can always go to a healer to make sure. Frankly, I think that would be a good idea anyway." He frowned. "You've been going to a human doctor?"

"Uh, yeah? Why? Is that a problem?"

He cursed. "It would have been if you'd had the baby

there. I know you thought I was human at the time, but since I'm not, and since you're not anymore, giving birth might be…interesting."

She held up a hand. "First, explain what you mean because you're scaring me. Then we can go back to what it means that I could die as a phoenix. It's a lot to deal with and you're going to have to go slow since I have pregnancy brain."

He kissed her palm before tangling his fingers with hers. "You're beautiful."

She rolled her eyes. "Thank you, now explain, kitty cat."

"I don't know what could happen exactly during birth, but you or the baby could exhibit some of your powers. The baby will be born in his or her human form, so no worries on a litter or anything, but they could roar instead of cry for their first sound."

She coughed. "Litter? Roar?" Apparently, she could only speak in one-word sentences.

"You're only having one for now, beauty," Malik soothed. "The next time you get pregnant since we'll be mated, there's a chance for multiples. It's how cats work."

She put her hands over her belly, pulling her hand from Malik's. "Let's just deal with this one first."

"As for a roar, yes, the baby could roar after taking its first breath. Between that and the fact that you could end up removing your glamour and reveal your true form while in pain and under duress…"

She froze. She'd been very careful not to look down at her arms or to the side to see her reflection in the mirror. She hadn't wanted to see what she was until Malik told her she was safe…but now…now she wasn't so sure that was a good idea.

"What do you mean glamour? Malik?" Fear laced her voice and her mate—her *mate*—leaned forward to kiss her softly.

"I'll teach you, beauty. You're a phoenix. Stand up and look in the mirror and I'll explain what that means and what you can expect. At least, what I know. We'll go to the phoenix realm as soon as we can so you can learn more about your people. I promise you, no matter what, you'll never be alone in this."

Eliana took a deep breath, knowing she'd had to trust him in order to mate with him, so she could trust him now. It wasn't easy, but nothing worth fighting for ever was. She stood on shaky legs, grateful Malik stood at her side, keeping her on her feet. The mirror to the side of the bookshelf on the wall was a full standing mirror that she used to make sure her outfits matched before she ran out of the house for one thing or another. She'd never thought to one day use it to see what she looked like as a phoenix, rather than as a human.

She didn't look too different, but she wasn't the same

Eliana she'd been before. The first thing that caught her eye was Malik's mark on her shoulder. It didn't hurt, but she could feel the warmth there, the promise of something more. Her hand reached up to hover over it, and Malik let out a satisfied growl.

"I don't think I'll ever get used to you growling and supposedly roaring," she said dryly.

"Get used to it. I tend to growl a lot." He let out another growl, this one deeper. "And I've never seen anything as sexy as my mark on you." He leaned down and licked over it, sending delicious shivers down her body. "I plan to mark you again and again when we're alone and you're ready. Marks just for you and me."

She closed her eyes and let out a groan. This wasn't the time for that kind of talk, but damn if she didn't want to hear more. She opened her eyes once more, this time taking in the fact that she was a new Eliana, not the one she'd been before.

Her skin glowed with an incandescent light that should have scared her, but instead, spoke of a power she would one day learn to harness and nurture. New tattoos inked her forearms, and she couldn't help but run her fingers down them.

She gasped when she felt not fresh ink, but *feathers*. "Malik?" she asked, her voice breaking. "Are these...feathers?"

He wrapped his arms around her and put his hand

over hers. "Not exactly. It's more like a brand of your history, much like the others in your group who have changed into paranormals with a type of ink. It feels like feathers because of who you are, but it's still ink. Skin. If not for the glow, you could walk around in the human realm with that ink showing and no one would be the wiser."

She studied her new brightly colored ink and couldn't help but pet it over and over. "My history?" she asked, aware she needed to keep asking questions.

"Each feather is your personal history, your family history...and your curse."

Her head shot up. "Curse?" she gasped. "Like Amara? I'm cursed?"

He shook his head before turning her away from her reflection and into his arms. "Not exactly. It's more of an additional...burden, for lack of a better word, your line carries." He frowned as he studied the marks. "I don't know what each means because that is something from your realm. In fact, I don't know if I've ever heard of a phoenix mating outside the realm before."

He looked up and into her gaze. "We will figure it out, beauty."

"But you said I could die."

He nodded. "Yes, but you can come back," he whispered. "That's the thing about phoenixes, they can come back. Your curse is what can kill you in truth."

She took a staggered step back, her hands over her belly. "I...I can't breathe." Her lungs seized and she couldn't get in enough air. "I...what happens if I'm killed but I come back? How does that work? Malik?"

He crushed her to his body and she grabbed onto him like a lifeline. "We'll figure it out. It's going to be okay. I promise you. You're not alone, Eliana. Never again. Do you hear me? You're not alone."

She leaned in to him, her belly making it difficult, but she didn't care. The baby kicked again, apparently wanting to be near Malik, as well. Everything had changed so quickly, and she felt like she kept running to keep up and couldn't quite do it.

Malik ran his hand through her hair and murmured in her ear, his warm breath soothing her as much as the words themselves.

"I thought I'd turn into a witch or maybe something that I've already met through the group. I figured we'd exhausted the amount of paranormals out there and I wouldn't have to go through anything too new or scary." She closed her eyes. "Boy, was I wrong."

Malik pulled back slightly to look into her eyes. "I think the Conclave wanted to see what each of you could turn into. I don't think they would have liked repeats."

Her eyes widened and she held back a curse. "I didn't even think about that. Damn it. Why didn't I think about that?"

"Because you're having a baby and we're dealing with the fact that I left because I was an idiot. You don't have to think about everything. That's what a mating is for. I can help you think."

She didn't narrow her eyes at his choice of words but it was close. Hopefully, the man would realize that he didn't have think *for* her but *with* her. One problem at a time, though, and since she couldn't quite figure out which one to wade through first, she figured she'd go with something out of the box.

"Will you shift for me?" she asked quietly.

He stiffened for a moment before pulling back to look at her. "You want me to shift?"

She nodded. "I...I can't think about everything at once or I'll stress myself out more than I already am. So can you shift for me? Show me what you look like as a lion? I know it doesn't make any sense, but maybe if I see you in your other form, it will make this all a bit more real. Because, frankly, this feels more like a dream than anything else right now."

He ran his thumbs over her cheekbones and nodded. "I can do that. Then I'll show you how to glamour yourself so you can leave the house and figure out the next steps. How does that sound?"

She smiled softly. "I think that sounds like a perfect plan."

Malik let out a breath. "Good, because I'm kind of

freaking out, too." He smiled sheepishly. "It's been a long day."

She snorted. "Will you stay?" she asked suddenly. "After you shift back, will you stay? We can figure out the next step in the morning." She was afraid if he left, he might not come back, but she wasn't sure that was all of it. She loved this man and wanted him with her. He was her *mate* now, and that made her feel so many emotions she couldn't quite quantify them. This man, this lion, was *hers,* and because she'd taken that leap, she had to traverse the world and this new path at his side, rather than worrying if he'd leave her once more. Because if she didn't do that, there would be no true happiness in this mating.

He was hers, and he was the father of her unborn child. No matter what happened next, she wouldn't be alone in dealing with it. She'd find out what it meant to be a phoenix and what the curse meant. She would figure out her powers and how to protect her child in a world where things weren't just light and dark, but also grey and far wider than anything she'd known before. She'd find a way to fit into Malik's life and realm. He would be King, he'd said, and she knew he couldn't walk away from that. He'd told her he had issues with his family and that his father was dying and there was only so long he could stay away from that. He'd left before for a reason, and now she would have to leave with him because there was no way she could stay away again.

Her life had changed in an instant with the lightning, and now it had changed once again. She was mate to Malik and soon to be a mother. She was a phoenix and an artist. She was still Eliana, but never only Eliana.

And because all of that was too much to deal with after a long and emotional day—especially since she was pregnant—she wanted to see Malik shift into a lion and back again before she passed out from exhaustion.

One thing at a time, she reminded herself. If she just did one thing at a time, she could make it. Because once the baby came, there wouldn't be another option.

Malik ran his thumb over her cheek. "Ready, beauty?"

She loved that he called her that. He hadn't called her that before, only her name. Now it was though he was finding small ways to be close to her since he didn't have to hold back as much as he had before. Or maybe it was just her putting too much emphasis on a word. Either way, he was *hers* and he'd have to fight her if he ever wanted her to let him go.

"I'm ready."

Malik grinned and took a step back. "I can shift with my clothes on and have them come back because of my royal line. The baby, once he or she learns to shift and gains enough power, should be the same. But we might have a naked baby crawling around for a bit."

She grinned at the idea, even if her mind whirled. It was scary enough to think she would have a baby, now that she was apparently having a *cub*, it just made it that much more monumental.

"When can lions shift for the first time?"

Malik frowned. "Soon after birth. I know I shifted about an hour after birth because I apparently wanted to curl up and nap, but it's different for each baby."

Thank the goddess she hadn't gone to a human doctor to have this baby. Because, holy hell. "Shift for me?" she squeaked.

He winked then glimmered out of sight for a moment. It was so fast she'd barely caught it, but one moment he was all sexy brown skin and man, the next he was a lion of such exquisite beauty it took her breath away.

He was larger than what she figured normal lions were. Much larger. And he had a black mane on golden fur. She'd known lions with black manes existed and had even heard a news report about a famous one at one time, but she'd never really seen one.

"You're beautiful."

Malik chuffed, and she figured that was some form of lion laugh.

She smiled and reached out to touch him, only to freeze at the feeling of an inward snap. Wetness covered her legs and she looked down in horror and shock.

"Oh, dear goddess."

Malik shifted back right away. "Eliana? Did your water just break?" Panic filled his voice and she couldn't blame him.

She met his gaze and clutched her belly. "I think so. I think the baby's coming, Malik."

She tried to smile, tried to think, but all she could do was freak out. Because she wasn't ready for this, and yet she knew no matter what, her life was about to change yet again.

CHAPTER 6

E liana had told herself she would remain calm once she went into labor and the baby came, that she wouldn't freak out, but she had a feeling she was freaking out anyway. She'd literally *just* run through all the new and challenging things in her life and she'd *told* herself that she'd deal with things one at a time.

Apparently, little squirt had different ideas.

Freaking squirt.

Malik had her in his arms and in is Rover before she could tell him to take a breath and not freak out with her. One of them had to be calm, and she would have preferred it to be the large lion.

"Malik," she gasped as the first contraction hit. Her friends had lied. All of them. There was no way the girls hadn't used drugs for these because this *hurt*. Her stomach tightened and something rocked through her before ending in a cramp from hell in her back. She was going to die. That was it. The first contraction, and she already knew she wasn't strong enough for the rest.

Some mother she was turning out to be.

"What's wrong? Does it hurt?" Malik cursed but didn't start the Rover. "Of course, it fucking hurts. You're having a baby and we're not ready. I'm not ready. But it doesn't matter about me. We need to worry about you."

For some reason, seeing Malik freak out like he was even though he was usually the one who was calm and growly and took charge calmed her.

"Malik, honey, I need my bag. And my purse." She looked over at him and gripped his hand. "I have a bag packed for the hospital and I need my purse. It has my phone in it."

"You can't go to a hospital."

She nodded. "I know. You're going to take me to your realm and they are going to help me." She only guessed that was the right course of action, but from the way some of the tension left Malik's shoulders, she figured that was a good plan to start with.

He gave her a solemn nod. "Stay right here."

"It's not like I'm in position to leave right now," she said dryly.

He didn't laugh, and she didn't blame him. They were both on the verge of a mental breakdown as it was. He left her to get her things, and she sat alone in his Rover, her hands over her belly.

"Okay, little squirt," she said as calmly as she could. "This is going to be scary for both of us, but we're going to make it through. You're going to come into the world with a mommy and daddy who love you." She couldn't help but tear up at that. "I'm so happy Malik is here for you when you come into the world, because despite what I might have muttered about him before, he's a good man. He's going to be a good daddy to you and I'm going to do my best to be a good mommy. Now, just don't freak out in there and we'll be okay. Let me make it to the healers or whatever Malik called them, and then you can make your presence known. Can you do that? Can you wait just a little bit more?"

The baby gave her a slight kick and she took that as an agreement. At least, she hoped that it was because she knew she sounded more than a little crazy talking to her unborn baby.

Malik walked quickly out of the house with her purse and bag in one hand and a phone in the other. She hadn't told him *which* bag it was, but considering Lily had labeled the freaking thing 'Baby Bag,' she figured he'd found it easily enough.

After he'd put her bag in the back seat and handed her the purse, he got into the front seat and started the engine. "I called Tristan. He said he'd let the others know."

She let out a relieved breath. "I was going to call Lily and have her start the phone tree, but Tristan is as OCD as Lily so that works. Are they coming? And where exactly are we going?"

She scrunched up her face at another cramp, but it didn't turn into a contraction. She kind of wished she'd been able to change out of her clothes because she was pretty sure she was ruining Malik's car as it was. He'd moved too fast when her water had broken for her to care about practicalities like that.

"I can't open a portal to get into my realm. We have to go through a warded area much like your wolf friend Hunter has to."

"So the lions are inside the human realm like the wolves are?"

He shook his head even as he drove toward wherever they were going. "We have our own realm, but the entry points for each realm are different. So we have to go to the edge of the forest for this particular point. There are thousands of entries to the lion realm around the world and this is one of them. The others will meet us there as I've already relayed a message to my hunters that your friends have permission to be there. Normally, they'd have to go through a process, but I'm a royal and it's about time I use that to my advantage."

Another contraction hit her then, and she nodded even as she held back a scream. "I'm glad they will be there," she panted. She reached out for his leg and dug her nails into his thigh. He let out a curse, and she couldn't help but feel proud of that. Because having a baby *hurt*. "I'm glad you'll be there, too."

He put his hand over hers and patted it. "Just a few more minutes and then we'll be at the ward edge. Just breathe, okay? Pregnant women in labor are supposed to breathe, right?"

She couldn't help it, she laughed. "Is that all you know about giving birth?"

He looked over at her with panic in his gaze, but with more determination than had been there before. "If I hadn't been a fucking idiot, I would have had more time to research and plan. But since I wasn't and we can't go back and change things, I'm going to freak out a bit now." He squeezed her hand. "But I'm not going anywhere. There's nowhere I'd rather be."

Tears filled her eyes and she pressed her lips together, not letting her gaze leave him even as he turned his attention back to the road. They might have had the oddest courtship to date, but they were in this together no matter what. It didn't matter that they were going about all of this backward. They were finally together, finally a couple with a future. And now they had another life depending on them.

They could do this—and not just because they had to, but because they *could*.

Malik pulled over near a wooded area and turned off the car. He had the Baby Bag on his back and her door opened in the next instant. After he'd helped her take off her seatbelt, he didn't immediately help her out of the car. Instead, he stared at her.

"What is it?" she asked, ready to be somewhere safe and near drugs to help her through this pain.

"I love you," he said firmly. "I love you, Eliana, my phoenix, my mate. I just thought I'd say that before the baby comes." He swallowed hard before putting his hand over her belly. "Happy birthday, baby."

Tears fell down her cheeks and she hiccupped a sob. "I love you, too, Malik." She couldn't lie to herself any longer and hold things back. "And I'm so happy you're here for his because while I could have done it one my own, I really didn't want to."

He cupped her face and kissed her firmly. "Let's go have a baby."

She snorted. "I don't think you'll be doing much of the having, Lion-O."

He winced at the nickname. "Cut it out with the cat jokes in the realm, beauty. They have claws."

She raised a brow. "And?"

He just shook his head and picked her up. "I'm here

for you to beat up on and call names during the birth. It's kind of my job."

She just held onto him and knew that this was one moment she'd never forget. Honestly, she hadn't thought about what it would be like to be with him forever because she'd been so afraid to fall. But now that she'd fallen, she couldn't help but think that this man would be there for her and the baby. She had to trust in that even if trust didn't come easily for her. The fact that it did now with him should scare her, but she was too worried about the baby to do anything about it.

She closed her eyes and leaned on him as they made their way through the wards and into the lion realm. Later, when she wasn't in pain, she would study the place where Malik had grown up and where she would evidently be raising their child, but for now, she just let him carry her and her burdens.

Soon she found herself in a private room that looked like a hospital room but much warmer, more inviting.

"We're at a healing station," Malik said calmly. "It's not a hospital since we're at the part of the compound where the royals live. We have personal healers, doctors, and nurses to care for you." He sighed. "I've spent most of my time away from you here. My father is two doors down." He shook his head. "I want him to make it long enough to meet his grandson or granddaughter. I don't even know why I'm thinking that since it's not like he truly raised me."

She gripped his hand during another contraction. "Tell me," she gasped. "Why didn't he raise you?"

Malik let out a breath and kissed her sweaty brow. "You should be focusing on yourself."

She shook her head. "I'm trying to focus on you and not the pain because, apparently, they don't have drugs for me." Something she was *not* happy about, but apparently her new body chemistry wasn't conducive to drugs —which they hadn't told her until they'd gotten her on the gurney.

"My mother died giving birth to me," Malik said softly. "I was the first born and father never found another woman to marry. As he mated my mother, he couldn't ever find another mate, and I figured that finding someone else to be with in that way would be too hard for him. But I think the fact that he lost the mating bond broke him. He ended up giving me to nannies and tutors so he could reign over the realm."

Malik took a deep breath, and Eliana reached out to cup his face. "You aren't your father," she whispered. "You'd never do that."

"But if you..." he stopped. "I don't know what I'd do without you."

"And you won't have to worry about that." She didn't

want to think about that at all, but Malik had his own demons. Just as she had hers.

Loud voices sounded from outside the door and Eliana frowned. "What is that?"

Malik growled. "I think I have an idea. Stay here."

She raised her brows and pointed at her belly. "Can't really leave."

But he didn't say anything as he stormed out. The man had to stop telling her to stay places when she couldn't leave—and, frankly, he just had to stop ordering her to stay as it was.

The noise grew louder, and Eliana strained to pick out the different voices.

"I don't care who the fuck you think you are, your furriness, but you better get out of my way before I get all pixie on your ass."

Eliana pressed her lips together to hold back a laugh at Faith. Her friends were there, thank the goddess. But, apparently, there was someone in the way.

"You little mongrel *freak*. You are not fit to be near the Leo or his family. Get out before I have you thrown out."

Whoever owned that shrill voice needed to get a hand to the face or something because there was no way Eliana's friends were going to be barred from seeing her. Plus, Malik had promised her the others would be able to be there. Maybe not in the room during all of it, but she wanted them there. No matter what she had said before about being alone even surrounded by them, it was all a lie. She was scared and wanted her friends.

She wanted the family she'd made.

"Aunt Prudence, you have no right to bar them," Malik's deep voice flowed over her and the baby seemed to calm down some. *Prudence*? Really? What a bitch of an aunt name. "I allowed them to come here for the birth of my child, and you will not stand in their way."

"Child?" the woman gasped. "You cannot have a child. You're not mated. You're just trying to get around the rules of succession."

"Get the fuck out of here, old woman. My *mate* is giving birth to my child. I will one day be the Leo, and you and your husband cannot change things. You're out of your depth here. But if you don't leave my presence right now, I won't be responsible for my actions." His voice had gone low and dangerous.

Eliana let out a breath as another contraction hit so she couldn't hear what happened next, but she was damned tired of doing this alone already. He'd better get his ass back in the room and that aunt of his had better fall off her high horse.

The door slammed open and Malik stormed in, his hands fisted at his sides. "Sorry I was gone for so long."

She held out her hand and he quickly took it. "What the hell happened?"

"Malik's aunt is a bitch," Faith answered as she came in with the rest of them following her.

Levi let out a breath and kissed his mate on the top of her head. "What my mate means is, it's taken care of. Now you have more than enough people in this room to make sure you and the baby are fine."

Dante walked toward her and leaned closer. Malik let out a growl, but she just squeezed his hand. "You're mated to him now," the dragon whispered. "The bond between a lion and his mate can only come with true free will so I know you weren't forced into it. But if you find yourself still unforgiving of what he did to you, let me know and I'll take care of it."

"Watch yourself, dragon," Malik growled.

The blue and black dragon shrugged. "I'm a prince, too and far stronger than you. If you hurt our phoenix here, I'll end you."

Eliana held up her hands. "Okay, enough with the posturing. I'm sure you all have mighty penises and everyone is happy with them. But for the love of all that is holy, stop it. I love Malik and he loves me and we're about to have a baby. We're not throwing our problems under the rug, but we are moving on from part of it so we don't flounder."

Malik glared at her even as Faith cackled and Nadie snickered.

"Dante really does have a nice penis," Nadie offered, and Eliana threw her head back and laughed.

Jace chuckled even as he put his hand over Nadie's mouth. "Anyway, we're all going to go out to the private waiting area so you're not overwhelmed."

"We're here for you," Tristan said softly. He looked over at Malik. "Both of you."

With that, each of her friends and their mates kissed her forehead and temples before leaving her alone with Malik. She should have felt a loss at their departure, but she couldn't, not with Malik at her side.

"They didn't really comment on the phoenix thing," she said casually.

"One thing at a time, remember?" Malik said. "I'm sure they're all talking about it now, and when you're ready, you can show off your new feathers."

She smiled as she looked down at her arms. "I guess I need to learn to glamour."

He nodded. "Thankfully, no one caught us when we were driving in the human realm without your glamour. I wasn't thinking."

"We had more important things to worry about."

He shook his head. "The baby is important, but protecting our worlds is just as important. I know that sounds like I'm putting our baby behind others but…"

She squeezed his hand. "But it protects not only our

baby, but everyone we love. I understand. We'll make it work."

Another contraction hit and she gritted her teeth. Malik ran his hands down her side and back, soothing her. She was so damned grateful he was there.

"About your aunt?" she asked once she could speak again.

"Later," he growled. Another contraction hit.

Everything went quickly then. Healers came in and checked to see how far along she was, and apparently, she was farther along than they'd all thought. She gripped Malik's hand with all her strength and pushed when they told her to. Tears streaked down her face and she felt like she was going to die if this baby didn't come soon, but after another hour of pain and anticipation, she screamed, pushing harder than she ever had before.

Malik cried next to her, kissing her softly as the healer held the baby out to them. Their daughter let out a cry that ended in a loud roar, and Eliana sobbed even as she smiled.

"We have a daughter," Malik said softly, his voice full of awe. "A daughter."

"And she's loud," Eliana added with a laugh. "And ours."

Before she could reach for her daughter, however, the door slammed open and a tall woman with a pointed chin came in.

"Your father is dead," the woman snapped. "Long live the King. For now."

Malik fell to his seat, his hand still on hers. Eliana turned her attention from the woman to her newborn daughter.

Holy crap.

CHAPTER 7

Two weeks of pure torture surrounded by bliss seemed to pass quickly for Malik. Too quickly. He stood in front of his mirror, trying to figure out if he should wear a tie for his father's funeral or not. It didn't seem like an item he should really be caring about in the grand scheme of things, after all.

His father was dead.

Malik was now the Leo of his people.

He was a father.

He had a mate who loved him.

And he was lost.

Soft arms slid around his waist and settled over his stomach. "You're thinking too hard," Eliana said from behind him. She rested her head on his back and he closed his eyes, relishing her touch.

"I can't help it," he said honestly.

And he couldn't help it. In the past two weeks, he'd had to deal with countless things that he'd never had to before. With his father dead, his people needed a leader. The others had given him two weeks to gather himself and his new family before he had to truly be the Leo in all things. The two weeks were standard for any royal line. In that time, normally, he would be mourning and working on his new life.

Yet he'd also had to learn how to be a father and a mate in that time, as well as deal with his uncle and aunt, who lurked far too closely for his liking. He wasn't sure what they would do, but he knew they weren't going to stand by and let him be Leo at his age.

He also hadn't mated a lioness so he *knew* the other shoe would drop soon.

He just had to keep going and protect his mate and child.

And Penelope, Pen for those who loved her, could break him in more ways than he could fathom, and he would revel in every moment of it. His daughter was magnificent. A proud little cub, who at this moment, was sleeping in her lion form in a bassinette near the king-sized bed in the master bedroom. She slept on as he tried to come to terms with the fact that he had no idea what he was going to do next, only that he had to do it.

"We will say goodbye to your father today," Eliana

86

whispered as she came to his side. He tightened his arms around her and inhaled her scent, needing her closer now than ever. She'd put her glamour on even though they weren't in the human realm. Though anyone could scent that she wasn't a lion, she'd told him she hadn't wanted to add anything else to the trouble that lay at his feet. So she hid her true self while they tried to reconcile the fact that they hadn't even had time for her to figure who or what that self was.

He was a selfish bastard, but soon he would take her to the others of her kind and help her find her place. He just had to say goodbye to his father and officially take the throne first.

"I don't know if I'm ready to say goodbye," he said honestly. He hadn't known his father as he would have liked to, but he'd still loved him in his own way.

"I'm sorry Pen and I will never know him."

He sighed and tucked her close. "Me too, beauty. Me, too. I suppose we should make sure Pen is ready to go with us."

Eliana scrunched up her face. "I really wish she didn't have to go."

"She's their princess."

"I guess it's a good thing we didn't name her Nala."

He swatted her behind and kissed her. His cat stretched, wanting more than just this touch. In these two weeks, Malik and Eliana had slept side by side as they found their rhythm, but they hadn't made love. As a supernatural, medically speaking, Eliana didn't have to wait, but they'd waited nonetheless. It hadn't been the time, but he knew that time was coming soon.

He needed her to be his in truth as much as he needed to know his place in the world and how his new family fit into it.

"Let's get on with it," he muttered.

"Don't wear a tie," Eliana said as she slid her hand over his chest and to the skin peeking out at the top of his shirt. "You look more dangerous without it, and for some reason, I feel like you need to look dangerous right now."

He kissed her, sliding his tongue along hers before pulling back with a groan. "We need to go now before I take you right where you stand."

Her eyes darkened. "Later."

Later.

MALIK RAN A HAND OVER HIS FACE AS HE MADE HIS WAY TO the large living room of his father's home. No, he supposed it was *his* home now. He and Eliana had been staying in a guest room there since the baby was born, but now it was his home. The funeral had gone well, if not quietly. To his surprise, no one had spoken out against Eliana and the baby. They'd seemed...happy that he'd found his mate.

Only his aunt and uncle and their children were against him.

He'd have to deal with that, though he truly didn't want to.

Pen was tucked in his arms, curled into his chest in her human form. Eliana had put her in a tiny grey dress that made her look adorable. With all that had been going on, he hadn't been able to truly reconcile the fact that he was a father.

This child in his arms was *his* child. His blood. A creation of the love between him and Eliana. He'd never been the sentimental sort, but damned if that idea didn't make him want to cuddle his child close and cry just a little bit.

Apparently, he was a tad stressed out over all the new changes to his life.

"I don't think I've ever seen anything quite as sweet as you holding Pen close to you like that." Eliana stood in the doorway, her dark black dress hugging her new curves nicely.

His cat arched his back, wanting more of her. It didn't care that they'd just buried his father and that he now had the actual world on his shoulders. It wanted his mate.

And frankly, Malik did, too.

"You look beautiful."

She blushed as she ran her hands down her arms, letting the glamour fade. Her inked feathers shimmered and she smiled softly. "I'm not used to this," she said. "It's weird to think I'm not human because I don't feel any different. Maybe I haven't had time to feel differently."

He moved toward her, rocking Pen slightly as he did so he wouldn't wake her. "I'm sorry we haven't made it to the phoenix realm yet. As soon as things quiet down here, we'll go. I know you could go by yourself, but I want to go with you. That's selfish of me, though. If you need to go with one of your friends, I'll understand."

She shook her head and ran her finger down Pen's cheek. "I want you with me. As much as I know my friends would understand and be with me, this is something I know you have to be a part of. I said yes to being your mate, and that means I said yes to all that comes with it. We can wait to see what happens to me and where I come from and who I will be. I'm also not leaving you alone while you're going through all of this. I never thought my life would end up this way, and I feel like I'm taking one leap after another, but that's okay. It's not what I would have expected, but I'm…well, I'm happy." She frowned up at him despite her words. "Is it wrong to be happy today of all days."

He leaned forward and kissed her, keeping Pen safely between them. "No. You can be happy today. My father would have wanted that. He might not have been the man

I wanted him to be, the man I needed him to be, but he was my father. I mourned him for all those months I was away from you because I knew the end was coming. The fact that he passed only two weeks ago is only a number. I'm yours, Eliana. I'm Pen's, as well."

"*And* you belong to your people," Eliana added. "You can't forget that."

"I don't. Won't. Not ever. I've been raised to know that one day I would lead, but you didn't know that when you met me, when we conceived Pen." He patted Pen's diapered bottom, but she stayed asleep.

"I signed up for it when I said I would be your mate. I might not have known all the details, but I'm not some flower that will wilt at the first sign of challenge. I didn't know what my place was or where I would be going in a world where my friends would grow into their powers and I would be forced to stay behind, but now I don't have to deal with that. They all took the hits as they came and found they were far stronger than they'd thought they were. I want to be like that, and I'll find a way to be at your side."

"You're a queen you know," he added. "Even if you aren't a lioness, you're still my Queen, my people's Queen."

She smiled wryly. "I wonder if the Conclave knew they'd be adding so many lightning-truck to the ranks of royalty when they changed our destinies."

Malik snorted. "Knowing which members were actually part of it, probably not. But I think this is a way of fate balancing things out if you ask me. You're all important, all part of more than one world. I think we can do this. Hell, I *know* I can be Leo with you by my side."

"Even if some oppose it."

Malik let out a growl. "The only assholes who oppose it are the ones that wanted my throne to begin with."

"Language," she said with a laugh.

He looked down at Pen. "She can't really understand anything, can she?"

"She's our child, so I wouldn't put anything past her."

"Then I guess we should keep Faith away from her because that woman curses a he—ck of a lot more than I do."

Eliana shook her head before going to her toes and kissing him softly. "I think we should put Pen to bed in her room and set up the monitor. That way I can put *you* to bed and take care of you."

Her eyes darkened, and Malik had to hold back another growl. "Are you sure?"

"I have been sure since I said yes to the bite," she said with an honest conviction. "I want to celebrate life and be with you in all ways, Malik." She leaned forward to whisper in his ear, her breath warm against his neck. "I want to make love to you, Malik. Let me love you."

"Always," he gritted out, his voice hoarse.

In a heated fog, he followed her upstairs and set Pen up in her crib with the monitors set. The baby didn't even hiccup a cry the entire time, and he sent a thank you to the goddess for that.

As soon as he closed their bedroom door behind them, Malik was on his mate, his hands on her ass and his mouth to her ear.

"I had planned on going soft and sweet this first time, but I don't know if I can wait. So this time will be hard and fast and fucking hot. Then I'll go slow until you're writhing under me in heat."

Her body glowed and she wrapped one leg around his waist. "Fuck me, then, Malik. Because I need you and I'm tired of waiting."

He let his claws slide out of his fingertips and he sliced open her clothes. She let out a gasp, but soon he had her naked and on her back. Since he'd put her on the edge of the bed, he knelt in front of her and threw one of her legs over his shoulder.

"I'm going to eat you until you scream. I remember how sweet this pussy is, beauty, but I want to make sure it's as good as my dream. Do you think you can come on my tongue? Make me so hard that when I fuck you we're both calling out in need?"

In answer, she reached between them and put her hand on his head. "Have at it," she purred like a damn cat. "Taste me."

It had always been like this between them, hot and hard and fucking perfect. But now it was different, as well; all of that heat mixed with emotions he could finally feel. The mating bond between them sizzled, and he knew she loved him, *felt* it. The fact that he'd almost lost this killed him, and he knew he'd spend the rest of his life making up for it.

He lowered his head and licked her clit before feasting some more. She writhed under him, tangling her fingers in his hair. He looked up to see her use her other hand on her breasts, slowly working herself up. He'd never made love to someone who was breastfeeding before, but he knew her breasts had to be sensitive. He'd fuck her hard like he'd said, but he'd also be gentle.

This was his mate, his future, his *everything*.

He savored her taste, wanting more. When he worked a single finger in and out of her, her back arched and she came by that touch alone.

"Trigger happy, I see," he growled before biting down on her inner thigh. She called out his name and he quickly shucked off his clothes, needing to be inside her. There was one thing they had to cover first, though. "We always used condoms before, beauty, and I can go find some if needed." He paused. "Well, we used condoms, but it seems one of them didn't work, did it?"

She shook her head. "If it happens, it happens. I don't want anything between us."

He nodded then covered her body, needing to feel her lips on his. She kissed him with as much fervor as he did her. Their hands slid over each other's bodies, touching, learning, exploring. He loved this woman and everything she held, and he was damned proud that she was his mate.

"Will I hurt your breasts if I play with them?" he asked.

She bit her lip. "They are *really* sensitive right now."

He nodded then kissed the top of one globe. "Next time, then," he said softly before going back to her neck and licking over the mating mark. She pressed her body close to his and he worked a hand between them to hold the base of his dick.

"Ready, beauty?"

"I've been ready for a lifetime," she answered.

He let out a breath before keeping his gaze on hers and slowly entering her. They both gasped at the feel of her surrounding him, but he didn't stop moving. He slowly worked his way in and out, going deeper each time until they were both sweaty and aching.

"I thought you were going to go fast this time," she panted.

"Give me a minute," he said through gritted teeth. "Apparently, I'm a little trigger happy right now, too."

She laughed before letting out another gasp as he moved. He kept his gaze on her, pumping in and out, increasing the pace until they worked together to crest the peak and crash down as one. The mating bond flared, and Malik let out a roar before rolling to his back, taking Eliana with him.

"We need to do that again," Eliana said, breathless.

"We will," he promised, equally breathless. "We will." Because damn it, that had been pure bliss. He'd thought it was perfection with Eliana before, but he'd been wrong. Between the fact that he could be himself and be as strong as he could with her now, and that he could feel the mating bond, what had just happened between them was literal ecstasy.

And he'd do anything to protect the woman in his arms and the child in the next room.

Anything.

CHAPTER 8

E liana was a new woman. Maybe. She sure didn't feel like it most days, even with the inked feathers on her arms and the extra glow to her skin. Sometimes, it felt as if she'd wake up from this dream and everything would be as it was when she'd been in Dante's Circle feeling alone.

Of course, then Pen would make a little cry and Eliana would know that this was her life now. She was a mom, a mate, apparently a queen, and a phoenix.

And frankly, she didn't know what to do with any of those things when it came to her future. She hated self-doubt, and normally would be able to squash it down in order to get on with the next step of her plans, but this was a little different. Her life had been completely uprooted, and yet it was mostly her doing. She'd been the one to ask for the mating mark from Malik, knowing it would change everything. She'd been the one so angry that he'd left, that she'd have done anything to keep him.

That might not have been the best motivation, but it wasn't the only one. She wanted him, and now that she could feel the mating bond pulsate between the two of them, she wanted him even more.

Things had just moved a little too fast for her, and now her mind was trying to catch up with the decisions she'd made and the ramifications of those choices.

She ran a hand down her ink and sighed. If she were honest with herself, it wasn't the mating or Pen that worried her. In fact, those two parts of her life were the most…steady. Even the idea that she would need to learn how to aid Malik in ruling the lions wasn't as daunting as it should be. Maybe that was because she'd watched her friends rise to the occasion and she knew she wasn't alone. It wouldn't be easy, but Malik knew what he was doing, and she had to trust in that.

No, the thing that worried her lay on her skin as a brand of unknowing and fate. Malik had told her each feather represented a part of her past, her line's history, her present, and perhaps even her future. Yet part of the brightly colored ink held her curse.

It told her how she could die and not rise from the

ashes—not that she knew if she'd literally rise from the ashes like the phoenixes she'd read about in textbooks years ago. Malik didn't know much about what blood ran in her veins because her kind were not only rare, but apparently so secretive it made them sound almost like myths to a group of people who *were* myths to humans.

It boggled her mind that she could be killed and yet come back again. Only *something* could end her life for all eternity. She just didn't know what it was. She swallowed hard and tried to push back thoughts of death and fate, though now that she was a phoenix, she wasn't sure she could ever untangle her thoughts from that.

"Are you ready to go, beauty?" Malik asked. She turned toward him at the sound of his voice and couldn't help but smile at the sight of him with Pen in his arms. He was such a big man, all muscles and strength, and yet he held their daughter as if she were a precious and fragile bundle of joy and hope.

Honestly, Penelope *was* all of that and more.

"I'm as ready as I'll ever be," she answered honestly. She moved toward them to run her finger over Pen's cheek. Her baby blinked up at her and smiled. It was probably just gas, but Eliana didn't care. Pen was her baby, her and Malik's baby, and that meant she was the most perfect baby in all of the realms.

Not that she was biased or anything.

"We can wait, Eliana," Malik said. "We don't have to go today if you don't want to. I'm sure we can find something to do here or even in the human realm instead of meeting the phoenixes."

She shook her head. "We already gave word that we'd be going to their realm." It was customary to do so, and frankly, she didn't want to end up like some of the other lightning-struck and inadvertently start a war because she didn't know any better. Some realms were a little... trickier than others. "Plus, there's no point in hiding from who I am any longer. We only took as much time as we did because of the baby and your new duties. It took forever to arrange for you to leave as it is. Let's just go, find out what can kill me, and come back so we can cuddle."

She said the last part quickly, and Malik let out a breath before leaning forward and kissing her softly. She loved when he did that—just a quick kiss to remind her that she wasn't alone. The fact that Pen laid between them gurgling adorably brought the fact home.

"We won't be going alone," Malik said suddenly. "I have my trusted people here in case my aunt and uncle try something during my absence, but I also want to make sure I have someone with us."

Eliana frowned. "Will the other realm be okay with that?"

He nodded. "I mentioned it, and frankly, as the Leo, they'll be expecting me to show up with a guard of some sort. Until we find out exactly what powers you have, if any, and train you to protect yourself, I don't want you and Pen out and about without a guard."

She scrunched her face. "I don't like the sound of that."

He cupped her face and sighed. "I don't like the sound of you being hurt because I wasn't there to protect you."

She let out a sigh but didn't say anything. He was right, and this was just another way that her life had changed dramatically since he'd first stepped into it.

Someone cleared his throat from behind Malik and she pulled away, ready to take Pen from her mate so he could use his claws on the intruder. She shook her head as Malik raised a brow at her. Apparently, she hadn't hidden her thoughts well and she hated that. She hated that her first instinct was to let a man fight for her so she could protect their baby. She would have to learn how to protect herself soon because this new life of hers left no other option. Not that they'd been attacked since they'd been there, but there had been such a nervous tension in the air since Malik had become Leo, she wasn't sure what to think anymore.

"Eliana, this is Jonah, my friend and our guard." Malik moved so she could see the man in the doorway.

She'd seen him before in passing but had never met him. He was tall, broad-shouldered and had the air of someone who took no bullshit. He also had a prosthetic leg but seemed as though he'd been using it for years; from the way he walked, you couldn't even tell.

He raised a brow at her as she studied him. "Hello, Eliana. It's good to formally meet you. Malik and I go way back." He smiled wryly and gestured at his leg before shrugging. "I lost it in a battle long before you were born. I'm just as capable as any guard."

She blushed and cursed under her breath. "Actually, I was thinking that you walk as though the prosthetic is truly a part of you. I apologize if I was staring."

Jonah. "You weren't, actually. I was just making sure you knew I will protect you and your child with everything I have."

She smiled then and reached out for Pen. "Let me hold her as we go." She snuggled the baby close when Malik handed her over. "And let's get a move on because the longer we stand here, the more nervous I will be."

Malik kissed her again before leading the way. Jonah brought up the rear, and for some reason, she felt immediately at ease with him around.

Malik must have noticed the way her shoulders relaxed and took her free hand. "Jonah is much older than me. And a jaguar. He came to live with my father when Dad was a child. Jonah was one of the ones that raised me. I trust him with my life."

There was so much she didn't know about Malik, and with each new piece of information, she knew she'd never learn it all. And that was the point. She wanted to learn more about him every day until the end of their days.

She looked over her shoulder at Jonah, who gave her a mock salute. She couldn't help but grin at him.

"I'm glad he was there for you," she said loud enough for the other man to hear it. Though really, if he were a shifter, she probably didn't need to speak up at all. Apparently, it was going to take longer than a few weeks for her to get used to living with paranormals. They all had such different senses and powers. Yet the only thing she seemed to have was this glow and new ink. Hopefully, she'd find out more today.

Malik led them toward the tree line where he pulled her through the wards the same way he had when she'd been in labor. Except instead of coming straight through to the human realm, she found herself in a new place full of light, white fire, and an energy she couldn't quite place.

"What is this place?" she asked though she already knew.

"The phoenixes arranged a portal to connect through

the opening at our wards for this journey," Malik answered. "They wanted to meet you."

Suddenly nervous again, she bit her lip and brought Penelope to her shoulder so she could rub the baby's back. Pen seemed fine, but Mom needed some reassurance. The phoenix realm had promised a safe journey and had wanted to not only meet her, but her mate and child, as well. While it could have been a trap to kill her off for not being a pure-blood or something, for some reason, Eliana trusted it wouldn't end in pain.

She didn't know *why* she trusted that, but she did.

"Yes, we did," a voice said from behind a tree.

Eliana froze, but Malik didn't look too worried. Apparently, having an inner predator helped sense when others were approaching. She was going to have to talk to him about that because she didn't like being out of the loop.

Two phoenixes walked toward them, each wearing a long, white robe. Both were exquisite beauties. Eliana couldn't help but stare.

"Hello, Eliana, I am Ripley," the tall woman said. She gestured toward the man at her side. "This is my mate, Thorne." The man bowed.

"Hello, Eliana, Leo, sir," Thorne said. "I am the King of our kind and this is my Queen. Welcome to our home."

Eliana smiled and knew this could be a home. Her skin warmed and Penelope let out another gurgle.

Ripley smiled brightly, and, if it were possible, became even more beautiful. "Oh, she is a darling. Let us go inside so you can ask any questions you may have of us."

Malik gripped her hand, and she knew she would be safe here. No matter what happened in the lion realm, she had another home. It was a weird feeling, knowing that so quickly after coming, yet she had to trust intuition. And fate. After all, it had brought her Malik and Penelope.

After they'd settled themselves in the couple's grand home with ornate furnishings, Malik ended up holding the baby as Jonah guarded them all. Thorne sat next to Malik, speaking of duties fit for a king while Eliana sucked up all the information she could from Ripley as if she were a sponge.

"So we really burn?" Elaina asked, a little nervous.

Ripley nodded. "Yes, if we die from a wound not of our fatal curse, our bodies burn, but we rise from the ashes, whole and new."

"And are you the same? I mean, are you different? Do you keep your scars? Or do you show up completely fresh and new? And what about your soul? What does it do when you're ash?" She blushed. "I'm sorry for all the questions. It's just...so freaking weird."

Ripley took Eliana's hand. "Ask all the questions you have. Honestly, you are the first of your kind and it has to be a daunting experience. Our children learn from a young age what they can do what they cannot. It's inherent." She looked over at Malik. "Your mate doesn't know much about our world because we work hard to make it that way. If the others knew exactly how we could be killed, or worse, think they could find a way to use us to not die from mortal wounds themselves...well, it wouldn't be good."

Eliana squeezed the other woman's hand. "I understand. I do."

"I know you do. You're one of us, even if you're mated to a lion." The other woman winked. "Fate doesn't usually provide us a true half outside our realm. Again, you are unique. But you are still one of us, Eliana. As for your questions. You will come back whole and exactly as you were before the wound. Though you will gain a feather that is the history of that rebirth. Thorne?" She called out. "Show her your arms, darling." She slid up her own sleeve and Eliana's eyes widened. "I've only been killed twice, so I don't have as many extra fathers as some."

The colors on Ripley's arms were decadent and she did indeed have more feathers than Eliana did. But when she turned to see Thorne's arms, she couldn't help but gasp.

The man's entire arms were *covered* in feathers. They reached up to his shoulders where the sleeves of his robe were bunched up, and she had a feeling the feathers covered far more than just his arms.

"I'm a warrior, child," Thorne said simply, though there wasn't anything simple about death. "I'm a good warrior now, though I wasn't when I was younger, when I was still learning." He met Ripley's gaze, and Eliana felt as though she were intruding at the love she witnessed there. "I have died for those I love countless times because it was—is—my duty. I will always fight for those in my realm and those I care for. No matter the cost."

Eliana's eyes filled with tears, and Malik moved to sit next to her. She leaned into his hold and reached out to grip Pen's little foot.

"That brings me to something that I should have said before this," Ripley said softly. "Jonah, dear, do you mind leaving us for a moment?"

Jonah stood where he was, and Eliana frowned. "Why does he have to leave?"

"Because, as the Queen, I can read feathers. No one else can because if that were the case, *anyone* could find out what would be our final death. I need to tell you yours so you can protect it, but it's best if others don't know."

Jonah let out a growl then but sighed. "I will leave."

"You don't have to," Eliana said suddenly. "I...I don't know why I know this, but you need to stay." She frowned. "Why do I know this?"

Ripley pressed her lips together. "It is because you are from the Foreseer line, Eliana."

Thorne let out a curse.

"What does that mean?" Eliana leaned closer to Malik, needing his warmth.

"It means that one day when you are comfortable in your skin, your sense of knowing will deepen. At least, that is the case for those of us born into this realm. But with that line comes a sense of responsibility that no one else faces." Ripley let out a breath. "Thorne told you he died for those he loved, but Eliana, you can *never* do that."

Eliana leaned forward but didn't let Malik's touch leave her. "What do you mean?"

"You can only die to save yourself. If you were to die to save someone you love such as Malik or Penelope, you might not come back. Your line doesn't have a true cause of death, but one of unknowing *because* you are knowing. If you die for those you love, you could remain in ash, never to return."

Eliana's heart sped up, and Malik held her closer, kissing her temple. "I...I don't know what to think of that."

Ripley gripped her hand. "I'm sorry, Eliana. It's not ideal, but it is your curse. All of us hold one, and we learn to live with it. I hope one day soon you will be able to, as well."

Eliana's mind whirled as they continued to talk for another hour or so, but soon she grew tired. Penelope had already fallen asleep in Malik's arms. They said their goodbyes to Ripley and Thorne with reassurances that they would return soon.

By the time they made it back to the lion realm, night had fallen and she needed to feed her daughter and deal with the normal routine of life. Because if she thought about death and a future in a realm where she didn't know when and if an attack would come, she wouldn't be able to breathe.

She sat in her rocking chair and put Penelope to her breast. Her daughter ate while Eliana rocked, trying to focus her mind on the here and now, instead of what was to come…or what could never come.

Malik prowled into the room and sat on the floor beside her. When he leaned his head on her knee, she ran her free hand through his hair, petting him like the cat he was.

She had her family, and though the others had told her she couldn't die for them, Eliana knew she would do it anyway. If the time came where she had to sacrifice herself for her baby, for her mate, she would. Because it wasn't a true sacrifice if she knew she would come back.

"You're not going to die for me," Malik said simply into the darkness. "We won't put ourselves into that situation."

She continued to pet him. "We both know it's not us that puts ourselves in that situation."

He leaned closer. "You're mine, Eliana. I'm not going to lose you."

She was his, as he was hers, but none of that could stop the sense of knowing that washed over her. The sense that her knowing would soon become unknown.

And that was far scarier than any form of fate and mating.

CHAPTER 9

Eliana's back pressed against the door as Malik pounded into her. She raked her nails down his back, needing to hold onto him but not able to fully grip him when she was so close to coming. He had one hand on her ass, keeping her up while the other slid between them to rub on her clit.

As soon as he touched her, she shattered, her body shuddering as she came in violent breaths. Malik growled as she came around his cock, his gaze on hers.

"Can you come again?" he panted. "I need you to come again so I can feel you squeeze my cock. Then I'll fill you up. How does that sound, beauty?" Want me to come inside you?"

She rolled her hips and bit her lip. "I think you're

going to have to try harder to make me come," she taunted.

They were both naked, sweaty, and exhilarated. They'd already made love that morning in the bed and on the floor beside the bed. Now they were against the door in the bedroom. At some point, they were both going to run out of energy, but apparently, being a paranormal also meant you were supernatural in bed.

Score.

Malik let out a roar before pulling out of her. She whimpered as he set her feet on the floor then gasped as he turned her around.

"Put your hands on the door," he ordered, his voice a low growl. She did as he said, and he pushed her so close to the door her breasts were pressed against it. "Now let me fuck you." He gripped her hips and pounded into her. Each time he slid into her from behind, her pussy clenched and she groaned. She knew they were being loud enough to wake the entire compound, but she didn't care.

This was her mate, and damn if she was going to be quiet as he fucked her into oblivion.

"That's my beauty," Malik groaned. "You're taking my cock and loving it. Your ass is so fucking amazing. I'm going to fuck that, too. Just watching your cunt eat my cock like this makes me want to come. But I can't until you come, so push back on my dick, beauty so I can fill you up. Fuck me back, Eliana."

She arched since he had one hand on her upper back, keeping her in place. He slammed into her again, and this time, she came, his cock hitting the right spot at the right time. Malik roared as he followed her, filling her up just as he'd promised.

With her cheek to the door, she couldn't help but smile. "If we wake up like this every morning, we might not make it through the rest of the day."

Malik chuckled roughly before pulling out and turning her around in his arms. Instead of hugging her, he slid his arm under her knees and picked her up. "I have late meetings, and Penelope is in bed after a very early breakfast. Jonah is watching her, and I wanted to make love to my mate. Now we'll shower before we go get breakfast because I need you all nourished up so I can fuck you again later."

She just laughed and let him carry her into the bathroom where he then washed her; very careful to get certain parts of her squeaky clean. By the time they were done, Pen was ready for her mid-morning snack and Eliana was starving.

Malik fried up bacon and potatoes with some eggs on the side while Eliana fed Penelope. It was all so domestic, and yet Eliana knew it wouldn't be like this every day.

Soon she'd go back to the human realm so she could finish up her art projects there and find out how she could connect her old life to her new one. Each of the girls had done it before, and Eliana knew she wouldn't be much different.

She'd also have to eventually leave the house and see more of the Pride. It had only been a couple of weeks since Malik became Leo so it wasn't as if she were truly hiding, but it was time to figure out how to live in this next phase of her life. She couldn't hide from her future forever.

And, of course, she wanted to make sure Malik wasn't doing it all on his own. He might think he had to, but she would be his mate in all that counted and learn to help him where he would allow it. And in places he wouldn't allow it, she'd figure out how to make that happen, as well.

After they had eaten, Jonah took Penelope from her arms and carted her around like it was the most normal thing in the world. Apparently, her daughter had both men wrapped around her finger. Not that she could blame Jonah or Malik, as Eliana was firmly wrapped, as well.

She'd been so scared about being a mother, and now she couldn't quite remember how she'd lived without Pen in her life. It was amazing how quickly that had happened.

"What's on the docket today?" Eliana asked as she finished up the dishes.

Malik rolled his shoulders, staring down at his tablet. "I need to meet with the elders about a few things and then I plan on going to the warrior bunker to oversee their training."

She nodded as she sat next to him, one eye on Jonah and the baby. She trusted the man, but she still couldn't quite let Pen out of her sight.

"Anything I can do?" she asked. When he didn't say anything, she sighed. "It's not as though I can hide here forever."

"I want you to," Malik said honestly. "Because I don't know what my aunt and uncle want. They've been far too quiet."

"Maybe they've given up? You're mated and have a successor to the throne already. You're the Leo. Maybe they can't do anything."

He gave her a look that spoke volumes, and she rolled her eyes. "They're planning something. I know it."

The French doors that separated the living quarters of the house from the royal part opened and the hairs on Eliana's arms stood up.

"It's time," Malik's uncle spoke softly. "You've been pretending to be the Leo for long enough to know you aren't worthy of the title. Step down now before it's too late."

Eliana stood up as Malik did, aware that Jonah was near them, but not close enough. He had Penelope in his arms, and yet she couldn't reach them.

This wasn't good. Not at all.

Others began to fill the room then, quickly and in force. She met Jonah's gaze and the other man brought Pen closer to his chest. He gave Eliana a nod, and she *knew* he would protect her child with his life. This was the part of her Ripley had told her about, the part that spoke of knowing. She might not know who exactly was against Malik, judging by the amount of people in the room now, but she *knew* Jonah was on their side.

She had to trust in that certainty or all would be lost.

"What is the meaning of his?" Malik asked, his voice deadly calm. "You come into my home where I'm with my mate and child and threaten me? You're not in line for succession, old man. You haven't been since I was born."

The man threw up his hands and spat. "I was second in line for *years* before you were born. You were a mistake. I killed that bitch of a mother of yours so she couldn't make any more brats, but I apparently should have killed you long before this."

Eliana let out a curse as the tendons on Malik's neck stood out.

"What do you mean, you killed my mother?" Malik's tone was too low, too dangerous.

"Exactly what I said. Your mother didn't simply die in childbirth, you fool."

You killed your Queen because you're a power-hungry asshole?" Malik snarled. "Did you poison your brother, too? Did you kill my father?"

The old man shook his head. "No, I didn't do that."

"But I did," Malik's aunt spoke up, her shrill voice sending shivers down Eliana's spine. "The man was far stronger than he should have been," she cursed. "It took *decades* for the poison to work and still he wouldn't die. He clung to life like the mangy cur he was. My mate should have been Leo, not you or that father of yours. We will rule the Pride as it should be. Pure and with power. Not with random scraps coming in to muddle the blood-lines." She narrowed her gaze at Eliana. Apparently, Eliana was the scrap in this case.

If it all weren't so deadly, she'd have laughed at the drama.

Malik didn't say anything for a moment, and she knew he was biding his time. There had to be forty lions in the room now, men and woman who were traitors to the throne and to his family. He'd been dealt blow after blow, and yet he hadn't lashed out. He was waiting because he knew he was outnumbered.

And Eliana wasn't strong enough to protect herself.

She just prayed Jonah could get Penelope out in time.

"I'll give you twenty seconds to get out of my home," Malik growled.

"You're a clueless idiot, not fit to rule the Pride," the old man spat.

With that, the forty lions shifted at once with Malik joining them. Eliana screamed and turned toward Jonah, needing to get to her child. But as soon as she turned, Jonah jumped...*jumped*. He was a jaguar, not a lion, and even with one leg, could run faster than the others, and could apparently jump faster, as well.

"Save the Leo!" Jonah called out as he smashed through the large glass window, his body protecting Penelope's small frame. Some of the lions chased him, but she prayed he would be fast enough.

Malik roared again, and she turned on her heel as he fought off four lions. He was stronger than all of them, including the two left in human form—his aunt and uncle. Eliana did the only thing she could and picked up a lamp, smashing it on the head of the nearest lion. She was stronger as a phoenix than she was as a human, but she still wasn't a freaking shifter. She'd fight until she couldn't anymore and pray that it would be enough.

Another lion swiped at her and she screamed when his claws ripped through her side. She'd moved just enough that it hadn't gone deep, but it still hurt. She wasn't a warrior. She was an artist and a mother, but damn if she'd let her mate die alone.

Others came into the room then, Malik's guards, and she prayed they were on their side. When the new group began to fight the other lions, she almost let out a breath of relief. They weren't alone anymore.

But it might be too late.

Malik's Aunt Prudence moved forward, shifting as she did, her intent on Malik. Malik had his back to the other woman and his attention on the other lions fighting him. If he didn't turn soon, it would be too late and Eliana would lose him.

Eliana did the only thing she could do.

She moved between Prudence and Malik, using her body as a shield. Maybe she wouldn't die here, maybe it would only hurt and Malik would have time to live. Or maybe she'd turn to ash as her kind did. She *knew* she was risking it all, risking her life and her future with this one action, but she couldn't *not* do it.

If she died here protecting the one she loved, she might not come back. She might not rise from the ashes.

When the lioness's fangs slid into her throat, Eliana knew this would be the end. There was no way she could survive this, but Malik would live. That would have to be enough.

Malik roared over her, and she felt weightless, even as his arms came around her.

He was worth this pain, worth it all. Because he would raise their child and he would be *Malik*. She wasn't anything less than him, but this was something she could do. She could take this risk because it was hers to take.

And perhaps she would come back.

Perhaps she would rise again.

Perhaps.

MALIK COULDN'T LET HER DIE but he didn't think he had a choice. Her throat was ripped out and his mate was bleeding in his arms, her life quickly fading. She blinked up at him, once, twice, then didn't blink again.

He had his hand around her throat, trying to keep her skin together, but he knew it was a lost cause. As soon as his aunt had clawed through that precious, smooth skin, Eliana had taken her last breath.

Before he could kiss her goodbye, before he could process what had just happened, Eliana's body erupted in flames. The red and white flames didn't burn, but warmed him before leaving him cold and holding the ash of the one he loved, the one he'd thought would be in his life from now until eternity.

The mating bond beat once before fading and he roared, his body shaking. In a fog, he stood up through the ash and shifted back to his lion form. He ripped out Prudence's throat with one slash and clawed his way

120

through anyone who dared approach him. His uncle shook against the wall, his face pale.

Malik would have liked to have shifted back to human form so he could scream at the bastard and tell him everything he'd done wrong, but instead, he let the cat take over. He slashed the old man's throat and watched as his uncle fell to the ground, clutching his neck.

His eyes bulged and he let out his last gasping breath, alone and forsaken.

Still in lion form, Malik prowled through the line of dead bodies around him. His people had lived, stronger than those who had opposed his throne. The only ones who perished were the ones who had taken the wrong side.

And his mate.

His beauty.

His Eliana.

She had died for him, died for his throne, and yet he prayed she would come back. The others had said there was a chance she wouldn't, but that meant there was a chance she would.

Before he could grieve, before he could hope, before he could find Jonah and Penelope, there was something he had to do.

He went to the balcony that looked out over the Pride and roared. His mane shook as he put everything he had into the roar. Around the Pride, every single person stopped what they were doing and roared back. Some fell to their knees while others bowed their heads. It was a roar of grief, a roar of power, a roar of the Leo.

When he was finished, he shifted back to human and clutched the stone railing in front of him.

"I am Leo," he called out. "I am King. Those that threaten our Pride, that threaten my family, shall perish. Know this and follow. Know this and live within the Pride."

His head still lowered, he closed his eyes, aware that others watched him. He had to leave soon before they saw him break, before he became his father and a hollow ache of the man he'd once been.

"Malik," Jonah said from his side.

Malik turned and ran toward the man who held Penelope in his arms. He put one hand on Jonah's shoulder and cupped his child to his chest with the other. He would *not* be his father. If the mating bond never returned, if fate had taken his mate from him in an ever-lasting sorrow of death and sacrifice, he would not allow Penelope to be raised as he was.

But he couldn't think of more than that now.

He couldn't think at all.

Because Eliana was dead, and he hadn't had the chance to prove to her that he was worthy of her sacrifice; that he was worthy of the mating mark she bore on her shoulder.

"Malik."

He froze and raised his head. Jonah blinked up at him and took Penelope from his arms as if he couldn't quite believe what he was seeing.

"Malik," the soft voice said once again.

He let out a shuddering breath and turned on his heel. "Eliana," he rasped, his voice breaking. "Eliana."

She stood before him in a long robe, reminiscent of the one Ripley had worn in the phoenix realm. A new feather covered her arm—fresh ink and a new life.

He tried to take a step toward her, but fell to his knees. He held out an arm, tears falling down his cheeks.

She ran toward him, sliding to her knees at the same time to end up in his arms. He crushed her body to his before kissing up her cheeks and temple. He licked her mating mark, his hands roaming her body to make sure she was there and that this wasn't a dream.

"You're back," he whispered. "You came back."

"I can't explain it," she said in awe. "I was here, and then I was...well, I don't know where I was. But I came back. I'll always come back for you." And with that, she kissed him. He slid his tongue along hers, needing her taste.

Dimly, he could hear the roar of the crowd, but he ignored it, his soul, his mind only for Eliana.

"I love you, Eliana. You're mine for now and forever, for this lifetime and the next. You rose from the ashes for me and for our child, and until the end of my days, I will show you that I'm worthy of that flame, worthy of your soul." The mating bond pulsed between them and he let out a shuddering breath.

She cupped his face and smiled. "I love you, too, Malik. And you are already worthy of me and everything I do. I'm yours from now until the end of our days," she said softly before looking over her shoulder. "Now I want to hold my baby and be in your arms until I can catch my breath again. Because what just happened? Talk about breathless."

He shook his head in reverence before standing up with her in his arms. Jonah handed Penelope over, and Eliana clutched their child close, murmuring sweet words even as she held out a hand for Jonah.

"I can never repay you," Malik said, his voice cracking once more.

Jonah shook his head. "You are my Leo and I'd like to think, my son. I would do anything for you."

Malik blinked back tears and met Eliana's gaze. She nodded, and Malik swallowed hard. "Will you be godfather? Will you be Penelope's family?"

Jonah smiled. "I would be honored."

Malik held his family close, knowing that he would be able to rule his Pride and find his own path with them at his side. He'd almost lost them once, he *had* lost Eliana more than once, and now he would ensure that would never happen again.

He was Leo. He was Eliana's mate, Penelope's father.

And he was home.

EPILOGUE

5 Years Later

Time changed in an instant. One minute, you're drinking a beer with your friends, talking about the increasingly scary storm outside; the next you're flying through the air with your body slamming into the nearest wall when lightning strikes. Or rather, when lightning strikes *inside* the room and hits you and six of your friends dead center.

Eliana looked around Dante's Circle and knew her life had changed the night the lightning struck, yet she wouldn't take that back for anything. Her life had changed again when she'd met Malik, and once more when she had her child.

Five years had passed since she'd risen from the ashes,

and as she ran her fingers over her skin where the glamour covered that new feather, she knew she'd finally learned to take the changes in her life as they came.

Malik kissed her temple. "Doing okay?"

She smiled. "I'm doing fantastic. Though I still think it's weird that we're celebrating Pen's fifth birthday in a bar."

Her mate rolled his eyes before giving a shrug. "She wanted to see all her aunts and uncles, and this place is the easiest place for everyone to meet without having to deal with going to new realms."

It made sense, and since her baby Penelope—who wasn't a baby any longer—was currently giggling hysterically with Hunter and Becca's Hazel, she couldn't really feel weird about being in the bar that had changed it all.

Lily and Shade were slow dancing in a corner while their daughter Kelly was dancing with Samantha—Ambrose, Jamie, and Balin's daughter. The two were mimicking the slow dance and laughing each time they stepped on each other's feet. That particular triad was in a deep conversation with Becca and Hunter as they drank and ate.

Hunter's friends had come with their twins Lavender and Raven, and Leslie and Hawke were currently on the floor with the twins, rolling around like lunatics rather than parents. Honestly, Eliana wouldn't have it any other way.

128

Dante, Jace, and Nadie weren't making out in their corner, but from the way they kept looking at each other, Eliana was pretty sure they were thinking about it. The only thing that probably stopped it was the fact that their twins, bear cub Luke and dragon Kieran, were doing a little dance in front of them. Of course, that dance turned into a rumble, and Jace sat up, trying to give Luke pointers about how to fight against a dragon. Seriously, Eliana never wanted that bear to grow up fully.

Faith and Levi were having an argument about something, though it didn't look too serious. Their son Colby chased Eli around the room with a squirt gun of all things. Eli's parents, Amara, Tristan, and Seth were trying to clean up after their little terror of joy, but Eliana didn't think that would last long.

It was funny to think that at one point, she'd felt alone. Now she had so many people in her life she could barely breathe. This group of mismatched paranormals, royals, and Alphas, predators, and sweet prey were her family, her circle, and her future.

Lightning stuck overhead, and everyone froze. Calmly, each of the seven women looked at one another before breaking out into laughter. No matter how much time passed, lightning would never be the same.

They would never be the same.

Each of them had a new life, a new future, a new path.

They would all have their forevers as they would always have each other.

And everything had started here in Dante's Circle, where nothing was ever as it seemed. Yet their worlds were just as they'd always wanted.

Theirs.

THE END

Find out more in Dante's Circle Reborn

A NOTE FROM CARRIE ANN

Thank you so much for reading An Immortal's Song! I do hope if you liked this story, that you would please leave a review! Reviews help authors and readers.

Thank you so much for going on this journey with me and I do hope you enjoyed my Dante's Circle series. Without you readers, I wouldn't be where I am today.

If you want to make sure you know what's coming next from me, you can sign up for my newsletter at www. CarrieAnnRyan.com; follow me on twitter at @Carrie-AnnRyan, or like my Facebook page. I also have a Facebook Fan Club where we have trivia, chats, and other goodies. You guys are the reason I get to do what I do and I thank you.

Make sure you're signed up for my MAILING LIST

so you can know when the next releases are available as well as find giveaways and FREE READS.

Happy Reading!

Carrie Ann

Dante's Circle Series:

Book 1: <u>Dust of My Wings</u>

Book 2: <u>Her Warriors' Three Wishes</u>

Book 3: <u>An Unlucky Moon</u>

<u>The Dante's Circle Box Set</u> (Contains Books 1-3)

Book 3.5: <u>His Choice</u>

Book 4: <u>Tangled Innocence</u>

Book 5: <u>Fierce Enchantment</u>

Book 6: <u>An Immortal's Song</u>

Book 7: <u>Prowled Darkness</u>

Book 8: Dante's Circle Reborn

<u>The Complete Dante's Circle Series</u> (Contains Books 1-7)

Carrie Ann Ryan is the New York Times and USA Today bestselling author of contemporary and paranormal romance. Her works include the Montgomery Ink, Redwood Pack, Talon Pack, and Gallagher Brothers series, which have sold over 2.0 million books world-wide. She started writing while in graduate school for her advanced degree in chemistry and hasn't stopped since. Carrie Ann has written over fifty novels and novellas with more in the works. When she's not writing about bearded tattooed men or alpha wolves that need to find their mates, she's reading as much as she can and exploring the world of baking and gourmet cooking.

www.CarrieAnnRyan.com

MORE FROM CARRIE ANN RYAN

Montgomery Ink:

Book 0.5: Ink Inspired

Book 0.6: Ink Reunited

Book 1: Delicate Ink

Book 1.5: Forever Ink

Book 2: Tempting Boundaries

Book 3: Harder than Words

Book 4: Written in Ink

Book 4.5: Hidden Ink

Book 5: Ink Enduring

Book 6: Ink Exposed

Book 6.5: Adoring Ink

Book 6.6: Love, Honor, & Ink

Book 7: Inked Expressions

Book 7.3: Dropout

Book 7.5: Executive Ink
Book 8: Inked Memories
Book 8.5: Inked Nights
Book 8.7: Second Chance Ink

Montgomery Ink: Colorado Springs
Book 1: Fallen Ink
Book 2: Restless Ink
Book 3: Jagged Ink

The Gallagher Brothers Series:
A Montgomery Ink Spin Off Series
Book 1: Love Restored
Book 2: Passion Restored
Book 3: Hope Restored

The Whiskey and Lies Series:
A Montgomery Ink Spin Off Series
Book 1: Whiskey Secrets
Book 2: Whiskey Reveals
Book 3: Whiskey Undone

The Fractured Connections Series:
A Montgomery Ink Spin Off Series
Book 1: Breaking Without You

The Talon Pack:

Book 1: Tattered Loyalties
Book 2: An Alpha's Choice
Book 3: Mated in Mist
Book 4: Wolf Betrayed
Book 5: Fractured Silence
Book 6: Destiny Disgraced
Book 7: Eternal Mourning
Book 8: Strength Enduring
Book 9: Forever Broken

Redwood Pack Series:
Book 1: An Alpha's Path
Book 2: A Taste for a Mate
Book 3: Trinity Bound
Redwood Pack Box Set (Contains Books 1-3)
Book 3.5: A Night Away
Book 4: Enforcer's Redemption
Book 4.5: Blurred Expectations
Book 4.7: Forgiveness
Book 5: Shattered Emotions
Book 6: Hidden Destiny
Book 6.5: A Beta's Haven
Book 7: Fighting Fate
Book 7.5: Loving the Omega
Book 7.7: The Hunted Heart
Book 8: Wicked Wolf
The Complete Redwood Pack Box Set (Contains

Books 1-7.7)

The Branded Pack Series:
(Written with Alexandra Ivy)
Book 1: Stolen and Forgiven
Book 2: Abandoned and Unseen
Book 3: Buried and Shadowed

Dante's Circle Series:
Book 1: Dust of My Wings
Book 2: Her Warriors' Three Wishes
Book 3: An Unlucky Moon
The Dante's Circle Box Set (Contains Books 1-3)
Book 3.5: His Choice
Book 4: Tangled Innocence
Book 5: Fierce Enchantment
Book 6: An Immortal's Song
Book 7: Prowled Darkness
Book 8: Dante's Circle Reborn
The Complete Dante's Circle Series (Contains Books 1-7)

Holiday, Montana Series:
Book 1: Charmed Spirits
Book 2: Santa's Executive
Book 3: Finding Abigail
The Holiday, Montana Box Set (Contains Books 1-3)

Book 4: Her Lucky Love

Book 5: Dreams of Ivory

The Complete Holiday, Montana Box Set (Contains Books 1-5)

The Happy Ever After Series:

Flame and Ink

Ink Ever After

Single Title:

Finally Found You

information can be obtained
~Gtesting.com
e USA
251120
006B/145